M000281773

For Dagna.

[signature]

The Many Lives of Samuel Beauchamp
(a demon's story)

by
Michael Siemsen

FANTOME

This book is a work of fiction. Any references to historical events, real people, or real locations are used factitiously. Other names, characters, incidents, and places are the products of the author's imagination, and any resemblance to actual events, locales, or persons, living or dead, is entirely coincidental.

Copyright © 2013 by Michael Siemsen
All rights reserved, including the right to reproduce this book or portions thereof.

First Fantome print edition November 2013
FANTOME and logo are trademarks of Fantome Publishing, LLC.

Manufactured in the United States of America
1 3 5 7 9 10 8 6 4 2

ISBN 978-1-940757-02-5   (Trade Paperback)
ISBN 978-1-940757-00-1   (epub)
ISBN 978-1-940757-01-8   (Kindle)

Connect with the author:
facebook.com/mcsiemsen * www.michaelsiemsen.com
mail@michaelsiemsen.com * twitter: @michaelsiemsen

Also by Michael Siemsen:

A Warm Place to Call Home (a demon's story)
The Dig
The Opal

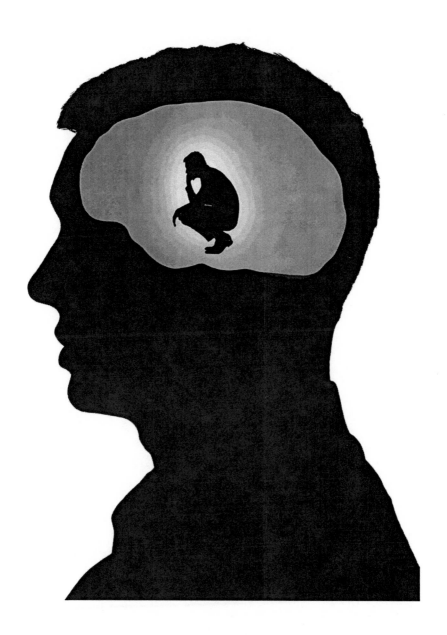

Table of Contents

The Many Lives of Samuel Beauchamp

(a demon's story)

by

MICHAEL SIEMSEN

O Son, how many bodies we must pass through, how many bands of daimons, through how many series of repetitions and cycles of the stars, before we hasten to the One alone?

- the Corpus Hermeticum

1. Tinker

My name—the one I currently use—is Geoffrey Cuion. I have lived in East Harlem, New York for nearly three years, moving here from Oklahoma City in 1956. I have a lengthy police record back in Oklahoma, Kansas, and Missouri. Assault and battery, mayhem, larceny, robbery, weapons possession, kidnapping, attempted murder, and manslaughter. Society would consider me an "ex-con," *if* society knew who I was. If they knew *what* I was, well ... that would be a wholly different matter.

My stocky body boasts countless scars—wounds obviously inflicted by knives and bullets—as well as a few minor burns around my legs. As the majority of ex-convicts claim, I had nothing to do with any of the aforementioned crimes, nor the incidents that led to my scars. I accept no responsibility for the "ROAD DEVILS M C" tattooed around a nude woman atop a flaming motorcycle on my right pectoral. Likewise, I did not select the vulgar tattoos on my right shoulder or left forearm. All are shameful vestiges of a life left behind, and I keep them safely hidden in public. The one thing I cannot hide is the thick, earthworm-like scar that runs the ridge of my jawline from right earlobe to chin. Though hair never grows there, I often knick it when shaving, adding scar upon scar.

I go by "Geoff." It sounds friendly, inviting. When people call me by name I light up. It must appear to the speaker that I am particularly elated to see them, when in reality it is simply an acknowledgement that I have them convinced. I am who they think I am. But beyond that, it means they do not know who I *was*. Well, who *he* was. Because they would have instead called me "Tinker," and being addressed by that name would mean that life, as I knew it then, was over.

Abilene, Kansas - 1956

I sat at the end of the bar and wiped the sweat from my pint of beer. Motorcycle engines roared outside Gracie's Canteen as the jukebox spun Hank Williams' "Your Cheatin' Heart." A wobbling fan overhead strove in vain to clear cigarette smoke from the air. A man in a crackled leather jacket and brown-tinted sunglasses sat at the middle of the bar, glancing back at the door every time it struck the hanging bell above. He had broad, square shoulders and little neck to speak of. His hair was greasy and long, slicked back and curling up at the neck. His big, bushy sideburns led to a handlebar moustache, and the right side of his jaw bore a large, raised scar stretching from chin to earlobe.

"You want sump'm, shitstick?" the man said, and I realized he was talking to me. I must have been staring, and with his sunglasses on, I couldn't see his eyes.

"No, sir," I said and looked down at my drink.

"Well, why you eyein' me like you know me? You know me?" Other conversations in the room quieted.

I shook my head and didn't look up. I reached in my shirt pocket, pulled out a dollar, and tossed it on the bar before heading to the men's room.

Wincing as the urine flowed into the steel trough, I waited for the pain to end. The burning down there had been growing worse by the day. A week earlier I'd had a bout of coughing, during which I'd spat bloody phlegm. Something was obviously wrong with Vernon's innards, and getting worse. When I returned his scrawny body to him, he would find his health problems well advanced, and would have no recollection of traveling from Denver to Abilene, Kansas.

The restroom door creaked open behind me, the garbled sounds of conversation and laughter spilling in. The door closed and I felt someone lurk close to my back. I buttoned Vernon's slacks and spun round to see the scarred man from the bar, his jaw clenched, lips crinkled tight. His sunglasses sat on his head, angry cobalt eyes wandering over Vernon's gaunt face.

"Pardon me," I said as I tried to move around him.

"You telling me to move?"

"Ahh ... yes, actually. Asking. If you don't mind."

His nostrils flared, he raised his chin, his neck muscles tensed into a bulbous V, and then he snapped into motion, slamming big, gnarly hands into my chest. My legs smashed into the urinal edge as my back crashed into the wall, a knob or pipe jamming into my ribs. My rear dropped into the basin, soaking the seat of my pants. When I opened my eyes he was arched over me. He grasped a clutch of hair on the side of my head and a switchblade clicked open an inch from my eye.

I had known he would follow me into the room. I'd expected some choice words and threats—something to goad me outside for a fistfight. The man was clearly scum, as I'd assumed, but if this was the sort of thing he pulled when someone merely *looked* at him, I was certain he'd done far worse in his lifetime. And I had seen enough.

I eased out of Vernon and slid into "Tinker."

"Tinker, what the hell, man?" a fellow in a leather vest gawked from the doorway. "Gracie gonna ban you for life this time."

I stood up and turned, washed my hands in the sink, then looked over my face in the mirror.

"You all right, Mister?" the man in the door asked. "Mister?"

I walked back into the bar in silence and strode across the room toward the exit, all eyes on me. Behind me, I heard Vernon's panicked voice shout, "Where am I?" as I raised Tinker's hand to pull the main entrance door, acting as nonchalant as possible. The bell overhead chimed.

I strove to curb my paranoid thoughts. *They know! Someone knows! Run!*

Outside in the hazy sunlight, bikers lingered around motorcycles and a stock car on a trailer. I pulled Tinker's sunglasses down over his eyes and walked to my new motorcycle, the one on which I'd seen him arrive earlier. I was relaxed, cool, but also tough and scary, or at least that was the impression I was going for....

Someone nearby called out, "You headin' out, Tinker?"

I glanced over and nodded, searching my pockets for keys. A tall man with spiked blonde hair and shiny sunglasses was moseying toward me. I found the keys in a breast pocket, mounted the motorcycle, and attempted to shoot a sinister look his way. He paused, peered behind him down the road, then took another hesitant step toward me.

He tilted his head. "Bird said he was gonna come talk'atcha over here. You likely wanna wait a while for him to show...."

I started the engine.

"Well, where's you headed?" he shouted over the roar.

I walked the bike back a few yards and throttled onto Highway 40, heading east, a trail of dust pluming in my wake. Buffeting wind beneath my shirt and jacket chilled the glaze of sweat on my chest. Tinker was a dirty, sticky man before I'd arrived, but my nerves and fear kept the perspiration flowing. Fear that a horde of tiny motorcycles would soon appear in my mirrors, speeding after me. Nerves about my stash—all my money and worldly possessions—stuffed into an abandoned well, covered with dead shrubs, all hidden beneath an old piece of plywood not twenty feet off an open road. And I fast learned that Tinker had actually needed to *use* the restroom—and *not* to urinate.

Exiting the highway onto the dirt side road, my rear wheel wobbled and slid. I'd had a bit of experience riding off pavement, so fortunately didn't fall. I glanced back down 40 in search of pursuers. None yet. The hazards and insecurity of body transitions had always been one of my primary reasons for delaying it as long as possible. And this biker I had chosen—an unprecedented risk in character alone: a public transition, acquaintances on the way to a scheduled meet-up, numerous witnesses to my silent departure from the scene, not to mention my earlier decision to leave my belongings in so open an area. Taking Tinker at that moment had been a rash move, a fear-based choice. And now I had to retrieve my stash in the light of day.

I dismounted the motorcycle and realized I was shaking.

I am such a coward, I thought. *Seemingly immortal, yet afraid of everything.*

My new stomach churned with stabbing pains, like an angry, violent criminal demanding release.

The wind shoved at me—quick, bursting gusts—like some invisible giant: intimidating, taunting, a thunderous voice in my ear. But the surrounding hills embraced it, their blankets of wild grasses dancing and bowing upward, pleasant green waterfalls somehow flowing against gravity. I inhaled a deep breath and let the peaceful sight calm me.

Such a beautiful world....

My gut reminded me that despite the world's beauty, nothing else mattered more than *release*. I was mortified by what I needed to do out in the open, not a shrub in sight higher than two feet, and cars passing every minute. I dropped my trousers and squatted, facing away from the road to hide my face. Sweat gushed from every pore as I heard a big rig (of course a big rig) barrel down the highway. I heard the brakes squeal momentarily, and then the ever-warping sound of a prolonged horn blast. "Just lettin' you know I see ya, buddy," it said. "Hang on a sec while I announce this over my CB...."

Defeated and ashamed, I cleaned myself as much as possible with bundles of barbed shrubbery and wide-bladed grasses, and kicked dirt over the scene. Relieved and re-buttoned, I stepped toward the plywood-covered well. And then my belly informed me that my relief had only been intermission.

A short time later I observed my stash laying untouched where I had left it. It certainly wouldn't have worked after switching bodies to ask a perplexed Vernon if I could borrow his car keys for a moment. "Just need to unload a few things, stranger." Especially looking like this Tinker character. In this body, I might as well have had a sign on my back that read: "Murder." No, when I passed Gracie's in Vernon's car earlier, I knew at once I needed to do a drop. There was sure to be body choices aplenty beyond those well-worn doors.

I lay down in the dirt and reached into the pit with both arms, grabbing my canvas clothes bag, money bag, then the crate. This was going to be difficult. I knew when I'd mounted the bike that I was making a decision to leave some things behind; after stowing the cash I'd amassed (about $280,000 at that point, primarily from an inheritance I'd arranged), the tasseled leather saddlebags would not hold much more. But I'd also been accumulating treasured *non-monetary* keepsakes for twenty-three years. I sat up and folded my legs together, squinting again down the highway. Still clear.

The crate first. I reached in and grabbed my Buck knife. *That* I would not be giving up. A gift from one of my fathers, a railroad bull named Dabney Fuller.

Early on, I'd lived as a young hobo named Rip whose life had simply been too difficult for me to endure. In his body I had been beaten, robbed countless times, forever walking a thread between hunger and true starvation. There was something about

Rip's slight body, or perhaps some aspect of my personality, that drew abuse to me. It was as though I exuded weakness.

In Cheyenne, Wyoming, I (Rip) had joined a band of younger 'bos (short for hobos) who, like me, had no families. We'd been waiting in the trees to board a freight, watching as a bull (railroad guard) walked atop the boxcars with a pistol in his hand, searching for folks between the cars. When they were gone, we rushed the tracks and climbed aboard, but the bulls came back.

"C'mon down now, you little shits!" one said, banging his club against the side of a car.

It had probably been a trap, but either way, we were yanked off at gunpoint and walked to the edge of the rail clearing. We sat for a moment while the other bulls hurried to come have a look at us. We could tell right away which one was the leader, because right after he stepped up to us, the other bulls' postures improved and they started chuckling to themselves.

"You search 'em yet?" he asked, floating a lantern across each of our faces.

"Not yet, boss."

"Well, strip 'em then," he said, and walked off.

"You heard my Pa, you tramper shits! Strip!" This bull was a fairly young kid. He couldn't have been much older than me, three whiskers scattered across his ruddy face and a uniform that hung off his shoulders.

The four of us stripped down to nothing, terrified of what might come next. "Fortunately," all they did was go through each pocket and hem, extracting coins and bills from every hiding place. I had thought for some reason they would forget about our shoes—

the toe of one of mine held twenty-eight hard-earned dollars. They didn't forget about our shoes.

When the bulls were done searching our clothes, they stuffed all of our money into a coffee can and threw our clothes back at us. The two grown ones walked off cackling, leaving the young mean one to "send a message."

While he beat us with his club, he called out, "Tell m'Pa to wait up fer me, all right! I's almost done!"

His name was Aaron Fuller, age nineteen, and he didn't beat or rob any more hobos after that day. Not after I jumped in there. That's the optimistic outlook on leaving Rip, but I'll share more about him later.

Despite occupying a taller, thicker body, I hadn't quite escaped the torment of others. Aaron's father was an extraordinary contradiction: loving and proud, yet rageful and volatile. One day he would embrace me and kiss my head and tears would well up in his eyes as he choked out doting, often poetic words, like "Yer better'n me, boy. Yer gonna *be* sump'em. Yer love is like a mountain on m'chest, boy." Other days it was as though a feeble dam held back a lake of wrath. He never balled a fist to me, but the rapid-fire slaps from his meaty hands nevertheless painted bruises and rattled my skull. He would scream, "Yer just gonna leave me! After everything I've done fer you! You never cared a lick about me!"

When I left, I was somehow able to slip from Aaron's brain without tearing his consciousness out with me. It might have had something to do with never quite feeling at home in him. I had always been aware of his presence there with me; he was a sleeping predator in the darkest corner of its den. I used this technique from then on when borrowing bodies, ever mindful of the *other one* with me. Aaron awoke in his home, frightened and confused, but then rapidly accepting, as if awakening from a too-real dream wherein he was beating a group of young 'bos. I was just relieved to see him awaken, and I didn't stick around to witness any revelations of missing time.

Another big rig roared past me on the side of the highway. I tossed Tinker's greasy dull switchblade and stuffed the Buck knife into my pocket.

Rubber-banded stacks of notes and letters, my Kodak 35 Rangefinder camera, the Mason jar full of coins and keys and trinkets. Everything had some level of sentimental value, but I needed to select a few choice irreplaceables that would fit, and then move on.

My books.

I was Jerome Johns for the early half of the 1950s, and it was as him that I lost my virginity, began my education, and enjoyed a few years of relative serenity in Colorado before events took a turn and an accident forced me to leave. My friend and mentor at that time, Quincy Holbrook, had given me many books: Graves's *Goodbye to All That*, Lawrence's *Seven Pillars of Wisdom*, Descartes's *Meditations*, Sartre's *Being and Nothingness*, among others.

I generally prefer not to think of Colorado. While I can attribute some of my highest highs to that period, the converse is also true. I would gladly give up many of the good memories of that place if the bad ones went with them. But this is not how memory works, is it? And so I do my best to bury the bad, highlight the good.

Over the years, fortunately, I had managed to disconnect my books from their associated memories. No longer did they trigger a series of recollections, but for the longest time I couldn't even look at them without succumbing to the weight of the past. They would just reopen wounds. I flipped to a dog-eared page and found a scrawled note: *"Strip everything else away … what do we know for sure?"* Quincy loved Descartes.

I don't want to talk about Quincy right now.

I closed *Meditations* and spread all of the books out side by side in the dirt next to Tinker's motorcycle. My fingers had flipped each of these pages multiple times, wishing I had a hundred more. I couldn't bring all of my books, nine total, so I selected four, wincing at the other five while consoling myself that many other copies existed in the world and one day I would have them again.

I opened my canvas bag and picked through the articles of clothing I had collected over the years. A hand-painted tie, an austere work shirt from the early 40s, coveralls. During World War II, I lived in a commune in New Mexico where we made clothes and repaired vehicles for the nearby town's residents. There I learned to ride and refurbish motorcycles. It was a peaceful pocket of land in a chaotic world, where no one exactly admitted they were avoiding the draft, but observing men forgetting their assumed names had become a regular occurrence.

"Hey, Bill, you on kitchen duty tonight?"

(No response, "Bill" keeps walking.)

"Uhhh … Bill?"

("Bill" stops, looks around, remembers these people call him "Bill.") "Oh, hey! What was that you were saying?"

"Kitchen duty."

("Bill" acknowledges he's on kitchen duty tonight.)

I can't tell you how many times I witnessed this exact exchange, with only a simple change of name and subject matter. It was actually rather humorous.

At the commune, I was a recent German immigrant named Anton Wiltzcheck. Ironic, no, that I was surrounded by others with assumed identities? It felt good to not feel like the only liar in town.

Apparently, Anton had not ranked high on the U.S. list for service, as they never called for him. We had no radio on the commune and were therefore successful in ignoring the imploding outside world. While it was peaceful, though, I do not look back on it fondly. The people there I considered friends were, in fact, just friendly. I was always an outsider, kept at arm's length and never truly trusted. Perhaps I shouldn't have worked so hard perfecting my German accent.

Despite the heartache, delicious foods were prepared in abundance there, and I had grown fat as Anton. Bread was my biggest weakness. I could eat it all day, and still do. And so began a pattern of my host bodies slowly swelling.

I had kept a pair of wide-waisted trousers I'd sewn there, and decided I would still keep them. At least one item from each life, I determined, and rolled the trousers, gathering a few more knick-knacks before returning everything else to the well. Perhaps one day I would return here. Maybe my valuables would lay safe long enough. The good weather would certainly continue for a couple months.

But I never returned, and rarely looked back.

With the motorcycle loaded, I gazed once more down the highway, started the engine, and rode south. I continued on until I reached Oklahoma, then turned toward my true heading: east to New York City.

The warm wind at my cheeks and hair, the smells of hot soil and big bluestem grass basking in the afternoon sun, I felt alive and ... *almost* free. There was only one problem—one sour nut in the bowl.

Tinker ....

Like young Aaron Fuller, Tinker was a furious, powerful presence in the back of my head. I had hated him within a minute. I didn't like what I was thinking about doing to him, but the more I considered it, the more reasonable and appropriate the idea felt. In my early days, "wiping" a person's consciousness had been an inevitable, unintended result of leaving their bodies. Later, I had learned to exit bodies "gracefully," keeping the original consciousness intact, and they had been able to resume their lives (albeit with some memory loss).

I pulled off the highway and found a quiet spot to park for a moment.

I'm sorry, Tinker.

Michael Siemsen

2. I was Samuel Beauchamp

Anaheim, California - 1933

Samuel Malcolm Frohler was born in May of 1916 in Anaheim, California. Descended from one of the town's original founders, Samuel's father owned a significant amount of land—land used for farming assorted citrus, avocados, and nuts. A year after Samuel's birth, his father joined his brother and brother-in-law as they enlisted in the U.S. Army to fight the Germans in the Great War. Fourteen months after he was deployed—much to the bemusement of those familiar with the typical term of human pregnancy—Samuel's sister, Esther, was born. Fortunately, perhaps, for all concerned (besides Mr. Frohler himself), their father died following a German phosgene gas attack in France.

Samuel and Esther attended Anaheim's Central School, the first school established in the area. Both were good students, complained little about their chores, and maintained a strong sibling bond envied by other parents in the community. Mrs. Geraldine Frohler had remarried in 1920, becoming Mrs. Geraldine Beauchamp. Grant Beauchamp had quickly gone to work erasing the past. He legally adopted Samuel and Esther and had their surname changed to his. Frohler Farms became Beauchamp Farms.

Mr. Beauchamp was from the South, where his family name had been regarded as local royalty. It was pronounced with French flair: *Bo-SHOM*, but such extravagance had no place in his new community. Soon, it was relaxed to *Beech um*, and the jokes receded. *Beech um* sounded downright friendly.

Many would later assert that Mr. Beauchamp resented his adopted son, exacerbated by Mrs. Beauchamp's seeming inability to produce her husband a male child of his own. This allegation would later come to bear in a sensational trial at the Orange County courthouse. A trial wherein a silent and expressionless Grant Beauchamp would sit accused of murdering seventeen-year-old Samuel Malcolm Beauchamp.

As the prosecution detailed in court, Samuel had been riding his bicycle to a neighbor's house two miles off a private dirt road, flanked by citrus groves on either side. Samuel would have heard the sounds of a vehicle fast approaching behind him. He would have known the distinctive sound of the truck in question, and the fact that the road only lead from one place: his house. Tracks and dents suggested Samuel had steered right to allow Mr. Beauchamp to pass, and that he had continued peddling the bike. But the truck didn't slow. It may have even accelerated. Samuel surely glanced behind him. The vehicle struck the back of his bicycle, mangling it and shooting it out from under him, and the back of his head slammed into the truck's large grill. His flailing body soared through the air as the truck skidded to a stop. His twisted body lay face down in the water runoff ditch at the side of the road. One of his shoes landed in the middle of the road, twenty feet away. Blood leaked hastily from his head.

Mr. Beauchamp exited his vehicle and walked to the front of the truck. He struck a match and sucked from his corncob pipe as dust wafted from the area.

The judge brushed off the defense attorney's objection to this blatant speculation. "He's painting a picture, Harlan. Probably an accurate one. Overruled."

The prosecutor went on, describing how Grant Beauchamp stared at the body of his adopted son and pondered. And the prosecutor had pretty much nailed it.

You see, this is when I had come to be. The moment I was "born," for lack of a better term. *I* was Samuel Beauchamp.

Much later I would learn the nature of this sudden ejection from my body, but at the moment it occurred, I found myself sitting several yards away from this surreal scene, low to the ground as if viewing the world from a cat's perspective. I could see a man I didn't know leaning against his truck, puffing from a pipe. There were two feet visible on the other side of the road, one wearing a shoe, the other a loose brown sock. Though I had no memories of people, events, my name, or of existing before that moment, the environment around me was not foreign. *These are trees. That is a man. Clouds, a truck, a pipe, a shoe in the road, a road.*

Curious, I wanted to see the rest of the body attached to the feet and so I moved—I *glided*—above the fine dirt, past the man's feet, to the ditch. I saw the boy's face coated with a shiny glaze of blood, his one visible eye wide, and mouth slightly agape as if about to speak. He looked surprised. I knew that he was dead, but I had no idea who he was, or how I knew what "dead" meant.

The man stepped closer, right beside me, peering down at the boy. I realized the man couldn't see me. There was an odd sensation—an energy from his foot and ankle. I looked him over and observed a strange blur surrounding his body from head to toe. It looked like the heat that rises from a hot road, but emanating outward in all directions. These waves seemed to be reaching for me, and they felt wholly comforting. Calming.

I moved closer, bathed in them like a thousand warm, wet, massaging fingertips. And then I found myself pulled into the man's body, thrust upward, and seeing through his eyes. The body lumbered forward, dropping to a knee. The hands hit the ground, keeping me from falling farther. I could feel the hands, the legs, the mouth. I could taste the sweet tobacco on the tongue, feel the sticky sweat on the back. I smelled the dirt, the trees, the sharp aftershave from the cheeks and neck. *My* cheeks and neck. *I* was in control of this body now.

"Hello?" My first word, addressed to the man whose body I inhabited. I received no response.

I stood up and looked at my dirty hands, clapped them together so the dust puffed off. I knelt and picked up the pipe from the ground. It was still smoldering. I brought it to my lips as I had seen the man do. Inhaling a small puff, I watched the embers in the chamber light up, heard the crackle of burning leaves inside. My throat was suddenly on fire and I choked. The pipe dropped back to the ground as I coughed, seemingly unable to get all the poisonous smoke out of the body. I wiped the tears on my shirt sleeve, took a final glance at the boy in the ditch, and climbed into the truck. The setup was familiar to me: *that's the steering wheel, the shifter, the gas pedal, the brake, the clutch pedal.*

I ran my hand over the bench seat. It felt how I had expected it to feel. The inside of the truck smelled the way I expected it to smell. I touched my face. It was smooth, clean. I put my fingers through my hair. The wet hair jelly stuck to my fingers and I wiped it on my trousers. It was unexpected.

I struggled for a moment, sitting there in the truck cab, trying to understand, trying to remember something, anything. The world was both familiar and foreign.

I decided to drive somewhere and started the engine without hesitation. My feet blundered about the clutch and gas for a beat, but then found the feel of it and I lurched off. I knew how to drive. I wondered if I knew because the man knew. A few minutes later I reached a crossroads, came to a stop, and my trail of dust caught up, sailing with the wind past the truck. The brown cloud drifted as an unchanging form and I thought it looked like a giant ghost.

Am I a ghost?

This question triggered a slew of disjointed, terrified thoughts. A ghost is the lingering spirit of a dead person. Why had I suddenly appeared at the scene of that accident? Was I the ghost of the boy in the ditch? How did I get into this body? Who was this man, and could he still see what I was seeing?

I looked both ways down the empty crossroad and decided for no particular reason to turn right.

I drove aimlessly for what must have been a couple hours, taking random turns, accidentally ending up in front of a few people's houses before turning around. Men in other cars raised a hand to me in passing. *That's a greeting.* I waved back. Another road ended at a large blue house. A woman and young girl hanging laundry in the yard gestured for me to come over to them, but I was afraid to talk to them. They appeared to know me, but I obviously didn't know them. I drove off.

Shortly after that, a siren wailed behind me. *That's a motorcycle.* Red and white lights shone from it. I held my hand out the window and waved, but the rider was clearly not just saying hello. He made his intention clear when he pulled up beside me. His face appeared angry and he shouted for me to pull to the side of the road. I stopped and got out. The young officer dismounted the motorcycle behind the truck.

"Mr. Beauchamp," he said as he approached. His voice cracked. He sounded out of breath, distraught. "You know what happened to Samuel?"

"Samuel?" My first time hearing the name.

The officer had his hand over a weapon on his hip. "Yeah, the Warren kids found him on the side of your drive."

"I don't remember what happened."

"Oh, you don't remember." The officer stiffened and moved his tongue around inside his mouth. I gathered that he was upset. "I been told to bring you in to the station. Why don't you get back in the pickup and I'll follow you there."

"Can I follow you? I don't know the way."

He appeared confused for a beat, but then his face grew increasingly angry; his chest swelled and deflated. I could see he wanted to do something to me—to hurt me. He kicked a rock, bared his teeth, spat to the side.

"This isn't a joke, Mr. Beauchamp. Samuel is ... Samuel's gone! He's dead, dammit!" He pulled out a set of handcuffs. "Put your hands in front of you, sir."

I complied, his eyes wild and watching as he attached a hot cuff to one of my wrists, then looked around the truck. He tugged me to the back, pulled my free hand between the slats of a rail jutting up from the side of the truck bed, then cuffed my other wrist. I had been attached to the back of the truck. He rattled the rail around, tugged on my arms to be sure I was secured, then walked back to his motorcycle.

"You're staying right here, Mr. Beauchamp. I'll be back with the other fellas."

* * *

Sure enough, the officer returned a while later with a car and one other motorcycle.

"Grant," an older officer said as he walked up and regarded my shackled wrists. He studied my face as he chewed the inside of his cheek. "You kill your boy?"

"I told him the truth." I pointed at the officer that had cuffed me. "I don't remember what happened."

"You been drinking any?" he asked.

"I don't know."

He shook his head while I glanced at the other three officers, all eyes condemning and filled with hatred. They walked to the front of the truck and examined it.

"Well, I'll be, Chief," one of them said. "Hit right there."

"Had to be the bicycle down here," another said.

The chief reached for the grill. "That's blood, I guarantee it." He stood up and looked at me. "An accident or you mean for it, Grant? Fess up now or it's gonna be a whole world'a ugly."

I shook my head. There was no point in explaining again.

At the jail, I sat in a sweltering cell with a single wooden bench and a metal pot in the corner. From their questions and conversations I began to understand the relationship between the dead boy, Samuel, and the man, Grant Beauchamp, whom I had become. Townspeople both uniformed and plain-clothed came to gawk at me behind the bars, fanning their faces and necks as they shook their heads and glared. More than a few made a disconcerting statement: "You're gonna hang." I somehow knew what that meant.

I would not hang, nor would I be killed in a poison gas chamber as still others had predicted. Mr. Beauchamp could have his body back, and then *he* could hang for his deed. As night fell and the jail emptied, I willed myself to leave the body. It was surprisingly easy, like stretching a thin rubber band until it inevitably snaps. I no longer felt the oppressive heat of the cell. In fact, I realized I sensed no temperature at all. Returning my focus to Mr. Beauchamp, I was disturbed to find he did not come to. He appeared to be asleep with his eyes open. I tried to bump him to wake him up, but found myself sucked right back into his body.

An idea came to me. I stood the body up, stepped to the middle of the cell, and slipped out. Even easier than the first time. The same blank expression remained, but he did not collapse to the cement floor. It took almost a full minute as he leaned progressively farther and faster toward the bars. His legs bent and the body crumpled down, his head scraping against the bars, settling into a knotty twist of limbs and bent neck and bleeding head. Still, he did not wake.

I had hoped that someone from the room next door would come investigate the commotion, but no one heard or no one cared. I moved up against the bars to try to get a look down the hall and slipped right through. I was truly like a ghost. I moved back into the cell, then out again. It was as though the bars weren't there at all. I could feel them, like the surface of water, but they did not seem to slow my progress when I willed myself through them.

I moved through the hall to the other room and found a few desks, upon which one officer lay asleep and snoring. His body had the same sort of waves floating from him. I wanted to go inside. They were calling to me, but I didn't want anything to happen to the officer. I didn't know if Mr. Beauchamp's strange state was my fault, or if I could use a body without doing harm. I waited until morning.

Mr. Beauchamp was discovered by one of the officers I had seen before. The body lay contorted in the exact same position it had been left. The cut on the head had clotted, and Mr. Beauchamp was still alive, though no more responsive than the previous night. Some of the officers tried unsuccessfully to stir him. They picked him up and lay him on the bench, threw cold water on him, jabbed him with a baton, and said with a pretentious affect, "Come on, Bo-SHOM, you ain't foolin' nobody." All for naught.

Mrs. Beauchamp showed up with the police chief a short time later. She wore a loose peach dress with floral embroidery, her dark brown hair clinging to her scalp in tight curls and waves. Her lips were painted a deep red, but only one eye had been encircled with brown makeup, as though she had been interrupted. She screamed at the shiftless body beyond the bars—her eyes red, spittle spraying from her lips. Her wrath unfulfilled by her inert husband, she threw herself at the bars, reaching with all her might, but still yards away. She tried to pry at the bars, clawed at the lock, demanded the officers let her in.

"You know we can't do that, Mrs. Beauchamp," an officer said.

She leapt at the officer and beat his chest and the others restrained her.

"He killed my baby! He killed my baby! Oooh, Sammy, no, oh no..." She trailed off and collapsed in the officers' arms.

* * *

Mrs. Beauchamp was driven home by Chief Claude Angstrom. I had followed her into the car and moved to the bench seat in back, but when the vehicle began to move, I did not move with it. I found myself floating on the dirt road where the car had been parked. I saw the chief was waiting to enter the road a short distance from me. A few vehicles passed. I rushed back to the car, moved through the side into the back seat, and tried to remain within as the chief stepped on the gas. I could feel the surface of the seat bottom and back, and concentrated on staying put. It worked, and soon we were traveling down the bumpy road toward the Beauchamp farm.

Mrs. Beauchamp alternated between quiet sobs and sudden wailing outbursts.

"He's going to the gas chamber, Geraldine," the chief said. "He'll pay for Samuel."

We turned onto a familiar road. A moment later, Mrs. Beauchamp began breathing rapidly and braced herself against her door and the dashboard.

She gasped, "No ... Is that ... ?"

"Well, shit," the Chief said. "I'm sorry ... I'll fetch it on my way out ... unless ... ."

"No, you won't," Mrs. Beauchamp said. "Stop, Claude. Stop now!"

He mashed on the brake pedal and I flew forward through the front seat, through the roaring engine, past Samuel Beauchamp's flung shoe, and then the ground. Though not *on* the ground, in fact, but *into* it. Everything went dark. I had fallen into the earth and couldn't stop. I passed through dirt, sand, and stone before eventually slowing to a halt. I was unaware of which direction was up.

I was horrorstruck. I had been buried beneath the scene of my body's death, never to resurface. It was meant to be, I suddenly believed. I wanted to howl like the woman who was once my mother. But I had no mouth, no lungs, no voice.

I tried to calm my thoughts. While I could not "see" in the traditional sense, I could perceive the environment around me. A dense stone layer. I moved a few feet without any effort. How deep was I? After a moment, I could feel the subtle downward pull of the earth. Once again, an up and down existed for me. I began moving back toward the surface, passing once more through stone, sand, and dirt. When I emerged, bathed in the light of day, the car rattled and clanked over me, continuing down the road. Samuel Beauchamp's shoe had been recovered.

Following the road a mile or so to its end, I found the Beauchamp farmstead, a bright yellow Colonial with matching barn and silo. On one end, cattle lingered on the other side of a barbwire fence. Opposite the cows, half a dozen horses milled about in a large pasture. Chickens and roosters pecked about the open field in front of the house.

The chief's car clattered past me, back down the road. When the noise faded I could hear Mrs. Beauchamp—my mother, I had by then accepted—wailing in the house. Inside, I found her sprawled on an area rug, deflated at the feet of a crying teenaged girl, a priest, and another woman whispering consolation on a maroon sofa.

I watched this scene for a while. Watched when they finally got my mother onto the sofa. Watched when she seemed to be struck by some revelation, her saggy moist eyes wide and studying the faces around her. She blinked at the teenaged girl for a beat and then reached her arms out.

"Oh, Esther," Mrs. Beauchamp said and pulled her daughter to her, cradling her like some oversized infant and moaning in her ear, "My baby, my baby, my baby … ."

Esther, Samuel's sister, had thin crescents of blue eyes and dark brown hair like her mother's, but hanging long and straight down her back. Sniffling and quietly sobbing until then, she finally released a muffled scream into her mother's abdomen. I watched as her whole body convulsed. I watched and wished I could mourn with them, only I was the one to be mourned, and I did not know these people. In fact, I was like any sympathetic stranger passing a funeral: *How sad for them* ... . But more, I yearned to "fix" their suffering. I wondered, and then dismissed the notion of finding my true body and leaping back in, gasping air, and apologizing for worrying everyone. But I knew my body was broken. It wouldn't be like raising Mr. Beauchamp from his strange sleep.

So what do I do?

I had no clue. All I knew was that I wouldn't leave. I had nowhere to go. Even without a single memory of the people or place, I knew this was my home and my family. I would stay with them forever.

Michael Siemsen

3. A Friend

East Harlem, New York - 1958

Despite the unfamiliar noise and bustle, the invasive scents and hectic pace, New York City felt like home. It appeared to me that this was the place where things were *happening*. Construction, technology, progress.

I had somehow existed for twenty-five years without seeing a single Puerto Rican, and then suddenly I was surrounded by a very different culture, often finding myself suspicious they were talking about me in Spanish. In the beginning, I wanted to learn the language just to assuage my paranoia ... or to confirm my wariness. But while put off at first by the sheer number of other races I would come across in a day, I quickly became acclimated to and less fearful of the Puerto Ricans, and the negros, too. They all seemed fairly intent on their work, entirely indifferent to my presence.

My work was at the Aguilar Library in East Harlem, and I loved it. My dream of one day having one hundred books at my disposal had finally been realized, but many times over! Granted, a large portion of our books were in Spanish, but it would take me decades to read only the English volumes.

My name was Geoffrey Cuion, Jr. (Tinker's real name), though I bore little resemblance to the man from Kansas. Gone were the bushy sideburns and handlebar moustache. Likewise, the slicked-back, shoulder-length coils of greasy hair. Instead, I wore a classy short cut, parted cleanly to the right, and a plain gray fedora when outside.

Tinker had poor vision and so I required glasses to see anything more than cloudy blurs. This is an interesting, unique aspect of my experience, being what I am, that might be difficult to effectively convey. Each person has been *themselves* for as long as they have existed. People needn't become accustomed to their bodies, because they are simply *me … myself*. In my case, however, there are traits to each body that I must adjust to. Strange pains, different strengths, sensitivities, allergies, hair growth. Transitioning between bodies with significant differences in size can be awkward—tripping over my own feet, or banging into corners I would have previously missed. And, of course, there is vision. I spent a retrospectively embarrassing week squinting and eye widening and straining to focus on objects only a few feet away. But I liked my glasses. I enjoyed appearing studious. I felt that I could speak with authority when recommending books to my patrons.

A shameful admission: my life was *so* much more enjoyable without Tinker lingering in my head. I often commended myself for making the decision to remove him from the picture. That quick, impulsive act afforded me a level of freedom I had never before experienced. I was able to enjoy all the benefits of human life, as well as those of my free form.

On occasion I would use this ability to excess, for no good reason—leaving my body to wander about unseen. Once, many months into working there, I even used it to remove a belligerent drifter from the library, leaving my body with its legs crossed on a table, hands behind my head, as if sleeping.

The man had been perusing the titles in the English Literature aisles, right hand down the front of his trousers, the other pinching his scruffy chin. He may have had an actual interest in delving into the classics, but I recoiled at the thought of that right hand emerging to reach for one of our books. Not to mention his steadfast odor was sending other patrons retreating to the exit.

I left the drifter standing confused a block away, babbling, "Who'sa where?" and he did not return. I was rather pleased with myself.

Other than my colleagues, I had not yet made any true friends in New York until a chance encounter in a bar called Mark's on Park. (I do hope I am not viewed as a habitual drinker, as it just happened that more than one key event in my life occurred in a bar. While I enjoy the taste of a draft beer, I seldom drink to excess, or with any sort of regularity.)

It was late March and the city's abundant Callery pear trees had blossomed early due to the unusually warm weather. I sat on a stool in Mark's, drinking somewhat to excess. Through the bar's large window I watched, amused, as the trees' foul odor turned the formerly placid faces of passers-by to scrunched grimaces of disapproval.

I had struck up a conversation with a clean-cut gentleman a few stools down from me. He wore a white dress shirt with a loosened black tie, cuffs unbuttoned and rolled up a bit. I figured he'd come here directly after work—perhaps some service job such as waiter or hotel concierge. He had appeared to be in particularly bad spirits, slightly balding head hung low and periodically sniffling. Though I did not know it at the time, his story, once wrenched from him, would forever change my life.

Following an exchange of empty small talk, I asked what had him down.

"You seem an awful nice fellow," he said, his wide-set eyes glued to the dark, glazed bar counter. "But I sure didn't come here to be laughed at."

"I would not in a thousand years laugh at you, my friend." I wore an earnest expression until he finally raised his eyes and looked at me, seeing I spoke the truth. "Whatever it is that pains you, I am a free ear, and have no right to judge another."

He regarded me for a moment. "Thousand years, eh?" He peered to the bottom of his empty glass, and then called to Mark, the owner and bartender. "Fill me up, Pops."

"I'm buying," I said, and Mark shrugged as he tipped the glass to the tap.

The man peered around the bar in search of potential eavesdroppers, then moved a few stools closer to me. He held out his hand.

"Stanley Bush. Call me Stan."

"Geoffrey Cuion. Call me Geoff."

"Queen, is it?"

"KWEE-on. It's French."

He shook his head. "Well, good to meet you, Geoff." He regarded me again. "You sure you're not going to laugh at me? I don't think I could stand for that right now."

"Cross my heart, friend."

He inhaled deep, took another look around the bar, and leaned closer to me, into the conical beam of an overhead light. I could see the fatigue around his brown eyes, a few days of stubble, and his short black hair looked like it could use a wash.

"My wife went missing a couple days ago."

"Oh my." I leaned back on the stool. "That's terrible. Why would I—?"

"Just listen." Confidentially, he continued, "A couple weeks ago, something happened. Something *changed*. With her. She was different. Forgetting stuff. Acting queer." I mirrored him, leaned in close. "I ask her something ... say, 'Have you heard from Frances?'... Her sister. She stares at me like she's never heard the name—looks up like she's trying to place it. I say 'Your sister? Frances ... your sister?' and she acts as though she knows and says, 'Of course my sister. I was trying to think of the last time I heard from her. It's been a while.' And she goes on about her business. But I know my wife. I know her faces. That wasn't the 'I'm thinking about it' face. That was a 'what the heck are you talking about' face! So one day, about a week ago, nothing's gotten better. I'm thinking she's gone batty, popped her cork. But she's still play-acting, you know? She really wants me to believe everything is normal. So's I test her. I says, 'Hey, honey, Pat rang the house today.' She keeps on ironing my slacks, nodding and waiting for me to go on. I says, 'Your Uncle Pat? He wants to bring the family for dinner next week.' And she smiles big, tickled to hear the news. 'Wonderful! I'll plan a meal for them!' And I says, 'You don't have any uncles.'"

He drew a swig from his sweaty glass. I wanted to wipe it down, dry it off. I never could stand the look or feel of condensation on a glass. I don't know what it is, like stepping in something wet while wearing socks.

I waved him on, eager. "And what'd she say?"

Stan's eyes drifted along the wall of bottles. "Her shoulders sort of dropped and she stares at me, blinking slow ... like a cat, and says ... she says with a nothing expression ... 'Well, aren't you the clever one?' and walks away, leaving the burning iron on top of my clothes."

I realized my mouth was hanging open and tried to appear more confused than fascinated. Whoever took Stan's wife's body was the first of my kind I'd heard of, up to then. There was no question in my mind that his wife had been occupied.

"Go on. What happened next?"

He turned to me, face unreadable. "Sound familiar?"

I stammered, "I ... Pardon me?"

"Does it sound familiar? The way she was acting."

"I ... I don't ... No."

"Pod people, man! Body snatchers?"

I hid a sigh of relief. "Right, of course. The film."

He studied my face. "You believing all this?"

"Pod people? I don't know. I mean, I believe what you say has happened. Why wouldn't I? What would you have to gain by fooling me? And if making me a fool makes you feel better, well, I'm happy to help, friend."

He shrugged in his defeated sort of way and finished off his beer, looking for Mark's attention. I swirled my handkerchief around his glass while his attention lay elsewhere. He glanced back, caught me red-handed, furrowed his brow, but blinked away his curiosity before resuming his account.

"She mostly ignored me for the next few days. And I was scared of her, so I stayed out of her way, but at the same time I kept telling myself I was crazy. Spooked by the movie, you know? But I slept in the guest room, handled my own suppers, and she never said anything about it. At some point she came in the room and asked me where we kept the luggage. Well, actually she just sort of demanded it. Said in a strange voice, "Tell me where you keep the suitcases and hat boxes." I pointed to the garage and she sighed, irritated, went off mumbling 'Who in hell keeps luggage in a dirty garage?' And the next day I get home from work and she's gone. I admit it, I was relieved she was gone ... but ... but I want my *real* wife back. She's an awful good lady... .""

He broke down at that, burying his face in his hands and crying. I pat his shoulder, but didn't know what to say. He sniffed and wiped his nose with a handkerchief, signaled Mark for a fill-up.

"I'm very sorry, Stan. I can only imagine what you must be going through."

"Yeah. I been sleeping on the couch. Can't sleep in our bed. Wake up with my neck and back all crook. No clue what to do with myself. Hadn't been alone for ... I don't know. Anyhow, thanks for listening ... buddy."

"Geoff."

"Right, Geoff."

He grabbed his fresh beer, stood up, and began gulping it down, obviously planning to go.

"Hey, Stan. Look, if you need someone to talk to again, I work at the library. The Aguilar."

He regarded me once more, but this time with what appeared to be deep appreciation. He snapped a nod, put on his hat, and exited the bar.

* * *

My yearning for acceptance and family and love had not faded, but I had accepted that such things come with time. Not only had I found patience, but the concept of family was no longer tied to stability and survival. I could take care of myself, I was employed, I had a home. It also helped to self-distract, to immerse myself in my studies. My chance encounter with Stanley Bush—what I considered confirmation that others like me existed in the world—refocused my attention on unearthing every indication of body transference in historical documents. There was much more to find than I would have ever expected, although discerning superstitious tales from true accounts proved a bigger challenge.

Over the span of but a few months of reading, I had discovered volumes of information on the nature of my circumstance. While I had always considered myself some sort of ghost with the strange ability to take ownership of a body—some fluke in God's design—I came to learn that I may not be so rare.

I had begun my research with the subject of "demons," the most infamous of beings that inhabit human bodies, causing the individuals to behave differently and speak in altered voices—often in other languages. There was much to be found on demons in religious texts, but while these accounts intrigued, they did little to satisfy my appetite for academic texts on the subject. They read more like town gossip one would find alongside childish tales of werewolves and vampires. And so I went back further, to the oldest roots of the topic.

I read and logged every historical mention of the human soul, ka and ba, angels, daemons, daimons, demons, strange spirits, shaman, witches, and reports of individuals with sudden altered states. I wished there was some way to write down a word on a paper, feed it into some slot, and have every instance of its usage spit out the other side! How amazing would that be?

I wanted to find others like me. I wanted to track down the soul that took Stan's wife, hoping they would be more knowledgeable than me, but also not a threat. There was no way to tell. From Stan's account, the individual in possession of his wife's body seemed irritated by and resentful of Stan, unsympathetic to the loss of his true wife, but did not ever actually attempt to do him harm. It was difficult to gauge how this entity would respond to me, if I found her/him.

I tried for many weeks to find Stan, frequenting the bar despite having no desire to drink. I couldn't remember his last name and so the telephone operators couldn't help me. There were apparently 3,400 Stanleys in the area. But one Wednesday, he just showed up at the library, looking for me.

"You probably don't remember me," he began. He looked marginally better off than at the bar, definitely fatigued, and, oddly enough, smelled of multiple colognes.

"Sure I do." I squared the stack of books on my cart and held out my hand. "From Mark's. Stan, right?"

He shook my hand while eyeing others browsing around the aisles. He appeared nervous. "Right. Well, do you have a break some time? I just need to talk, if it's no trouble. You had said—"

"No trouble at all." I hid my zeal and offered to meet him at a diner down the block at lunchtime. He agreed, thanked me, and glanced down at the topmost book on my cart, *Early Zoroastrianism*, a 1913 volume by James Hope Moulton that I had found referenced in a later text.

"Moulton, eh? Heady stuff." He turned to go.

I, astounded, asked, "You know Moulton?"

He shrugged. "Not intimately, but we dipped our toes in early monotheism in theology classes. I'll see you in an hour?"

I nodded and waved as he went.

That was when I decided: Stan would be a friend.

* * *

I met Stan at the diner and he apologized for the unannounced visit. We were both a bit awkward, neither of us enjoying the uninhibitive benefits of inebriation. He carried a lunchbox with him to the table, placed it on the seat beside him. He ordered only a glass of water. I offered to buy him lunch but he refused.

When he didn't initiate conversation I began by asking if he ever ended up hearing from his wife.

"Not a lick. Her family is just as foxed as me. I didn't tell them she had been acting strange, though. Didn't want to have to go into detail there. The police wanted to know if anything had changed before she left. If I suspected her of infidelity. They searched the house a bunch of times. I know what they think."

"That you did something to her?"

He nodded and searched my eyes, perhaps wondering if I, too, suspected him of anything.

My tuna sandwich arrived and Stan pulled a Thermos from his lunchbox, pouring what appeared to be split pea soup into the bowl lid. I noticed the irritated look from our waitress.

He peered up at me, caught me watching. "It's my favorite soup. I have it most every day."

After a brief lull, Stan wiped his mouth on his sleeve. "I wanted to tell you that I don't think my wife was what I said. I believe in God, and I know that movies aren't real." I nodded and continued eating, waiting for him to go on. He surveyed the restaurant. "It's awful quiet in here." He sucked in a breath, screwed up some courage. "I know ... I *think* I know what happened to her. And if I find her or she comes back with, well, comes back the *same*, I know where to go. I talked to a priest at Saint Pat's."

Stan didn't seem to enjoy eye contact, his head always hung low, but he would occasionally glance up with only his eyes to measure my reaction or see if I was still paying attention. I could tell he wasn't comfortable speaking of personal things.

"What did he say?" I asked.

"He said it sounded like what I thought." An upward glance. "You know what I'm talking about?"

I peered around and whispered, "A demon?"

He held his breath and swallowed, his eyes darting around the table. The word was not to be spoken. He snapped a little nod.

"You think I'm crazy? Father Will didn't think so. He asked a bunch of questions and told me what I needed to do. How the church can help. He believed me."

"I believe you," I said. "I absolutely do."

He raised his chin, looked me square in the face. "Why? Why would you?"

It sounded like bait at first, as if he had recognized what I was, but I knew this was my own paranoia. Of course his story would be unbelievable to most rational people, and my all-too-willing acceptance may have come too easily.

"As I said before, Stan. I don't know what the cause was, and I'm not qualified to suggest any answers, but I believe what you say happened. That she changed ... wasn't herself."

I noticed Stan's ice water glass begin to sweat and forced myself to disregard it.

He slurped his soup. "Then you don't believe it's ... what you just said."

"How could I know?"

"Do you believe that that sort of thing could exist?"

"I think anything's possible."

"That's a baloney answer. That's what moms say when they don't want to tell their children that what they're talking about is nonsense. It's all right, though. I mean ..." He smiled a little. A crooked smirk, the first time I had observed it. "... I know it's loony. If I hadn't seen it myself ... lived it ... We were trying for a baby." He sucked in a quavering breath.

I didn't know how I could possibly console him. I wanted to tell him my own story, but what would it help? He would fear me—think he was surrounded by demons! He'd sick the exorcists on me. All I could do was listen and tell him I didn't think he was crazy, though I did wonder if an exorcist could have any effect on me. But the latter was a curiosity I would not seek to satisfy.

"You work at the library long?" A relieving shift of subjects.

"Not particularly. Nearly a year. I started out volunteering and they offered me part-time employment a month later. I'm in school, too."

He perked up. "Oh yeah? What are you studying?"

"Philosophy and divinity right now."

He humphed and lifted an eyebrow. "You want to be a priest or something?"

"No, not really. My interest is purely academic. Though I may wish to teach one day."

Stan nodded as he wiped his bowl clean with a napkin, then screwed it back onto the Thermos. "Listen, Geoff, I have to get back to work. It was good talking to you. Maybe we can get a drink again sometime?"

"Sure, I'd like that," I said as I pulled a pen from my shirt pocket. I wasn't going to let him leave again without getting his information. "What's your telephone number?"

"Oh, I don't have one at my new place. Can't afford it right now. If you give me yours, though I'll call you from my work."

I wrote down my number and slid it to him. I needed to know *some* way to reach him. "Well, where do you work?"

He didn't like this question, his eyes shooting from the sheet of paper to my face.

I tried to backpedal. "I mean, what part of town? Around here?"

He gathered his things and stood up, stepped beside my seat and leaned to me, hushing, "I work in a commode, all right? Six days a week. Off Mondays. You know the Metropolitan Club? On Sixtieth and Fifth?"

Thus the wafting essence of numerous men's fragrances...

"I believe I've heard of it. Nothing wrong with an honest living."

He straightened up. "Who said there was anything wrong with it?"

"I ... ."

"I'll see you around, all right? I'll call you."

And off he went. I felt like a fool. He must have thought me judgmental, when all I wanted was to allay any fears that I would look down on him. Instead, that's exactly how it appeared.

* * *

A few months passed, Stan and I getting together with increasing frequency. We had grown more used to each other—more comfortable—and I no longer felt awkward in his presence. Each Friday night we played gin in the backroom of Caswells Pub in Williamsbridge with an ever-rotating group of guys. The two of us had also established a regular lunch date on Wednesdays at the diner near the library.

While Stan had only a private high school education, he was an avid reader of history. Oftentimes, he would surprise me with a tidbit of information he had picked up in a book, occasionally revealing an even deeper understanding of a historical figure or a particular culture. I found myself constantly stifling the desire to ask him why he never pursued higher education or sought a career that would better exploit his intelligence and knowledge. To do so, I lamented, would once more suggest I held a critical outlook on his job or lack of accomplishment. But what a waste! He spent eight hours a day, six days a week, handing out towels, offering mints and colognes, drying sinks, and refreshing toilets after each use! Granted, with his tips he pulled in more money than I did, but what of intellectual fulfillment? I suppose he was able to indulge with me whatever cravings he held in that arena, and likewise, I enjoyed sharing with him works I had unearthed, and having him read through my papers before turning them in.

The biggest turning point in our friendship came one night at his tidy, albeit over-furnished, apartment in West Bronx (he had apparently tried to fit as much furniture from his old house as possible). His living room had no less than six unmatched lamps and two extra couches pushed up against a wall. His kitchenette area sported three full dressers being used as houseplant stands. I never went in his bedroom, but imagined a similar situation.

Stan ironed his work suits while I read from Ernst Bösegut's *Exile of the Soul*. I had been slowly introducing him to my findings on historical daimons by sharing strategically random excerpts.

"Tell me I'm not crazy here, Stan. If we take these accounts literally, listen ... 'the presence of the eidola, so numerous as to be countless, and yet only perceptible to Clytemnestra, who herself too proclaimed proudly the arrival of her eidolon, and all at once the character of those assembled was transformed, once stone ears now sympathetic to the Trojan plight.'"

Stan spread the next pair of pants atop the ironing board. "Was that one sentence?"

I laughed. "Yes. They were a bit longwinded, trying to express an entire thought in a single sentence, lest you wrongly think a period means a new subject has begun, when in fact—"

He chuckled. "I get it! So you think this Clymenestra was taken over by a demon?"

"Clytemnestra. A *daimon*, yes. Along with this whole crowd of nobles. Think about it! This insane war is being fought, people hate each other. Thousands upon thousands of souls rise from the dead—some ascend to heaven, others do not. They float to the base where the leaders are gathered, take over their bodies, and suddenly the conflict ends."

"I don't know, Geoff. You think maybe you take these old myths too literally?"

"That's exactly what I do." I waved *The Odyssey* in the air before me. "Treat everything as a history book, extract consistent stories, make connections. You know there are two wildly different accounts of Clytemnestra? Homer has her as weak and submissive. Aeschylus's version is a callous manipulator who murdered her own husband. Before and after? How often do people's entire personalities change?"

"It is interesting. It's just so ... *old*. I wish you could find something more recent."

"Empedocles—"

"He's still three thousand some odd years!"

"No, just think about this." I knew what I was doing, where I needed the conversation to steer. "Empedocles declared to the world—*his* world, where he was well-known and respected as a speaker, thinker, politician—told them all 'I was once already boy and girl.' He records this for the ages: 'There is ... a decree of the Gods of old ... that when a daimon has sinfully stained his hands with blood ... he must wander thrice ten thousand seasons away from the blessed, being born throughout all time in all manner of mortal forms, passing from one troublous path to the next...'.'"

Stan smirked. "Troublous? I'm going to use that."

I ignored him. "'Of these I am now also one, an exile from the gods and a wanderer, having put my trust in raving strife.'" I stabbed the page with my finger. "He told everyone that he was a daimon, cursed to live on in 'unfamiliar tunics of the flesh' because of his sins. Pretty vivid, right? And think about the audacity! This is a super respected guy! Can you imagine if someone did that today? Like the mayor ... or a Pulitzer Prize winner?"

Stan began hanging his slacks in the closet. "Different times. In his world people still believed in all sorts of gods and demigods, every aspect of life manipulated by these chess-playing super people. Heck, today there could be people out there announcing they're demons or whatever all the time. But they'd just be hauled off to the looney bin. No one would believe them."

"Would you?" I looked him square in the face, not a hint of jest. "If they weren't the street corner raving sort, just a normal person. Would you believe them, what with your wife and all?"

Stan stood still and gave me a funny look out the side of his eyes. We remained silent for a beat.

"You got something you been wanting to tell me, Geoff?"

* * *

Stan did not accept my admission outright. I would have been shocked if he had. But his experience with his wife had opened wide what would otherwise have been a typically closed, rational mind. Interestingly enough, he did not at first mistake my confession for a joke. I suppose I am not the jokey sort, and any attempt to make light of the tragic loss of his wife would have been in extremely poor taste—tact being another of my apparent assets. So Stan appeared understandably perplexed.

"I'm not sure what to say."

"You can say you don't believe me. It wouldn't be out of line. This is not a normal conversation."

He continued to regard me. "I'm not prepared to say that just yet." He paced slowly around his apartment, running his fingers over the back of the couch and the crackled leather chair, his gaze locked on me. "Why are you telling me this?"

"Because you're my friend. I've never mentioned it to another soul ... so to speak."

"I'm honored," he said drily.

He reversed direction and followed his steps back round the room.

"Tell me what you're thinking," I said. "This is obviously a big deal for me."

"Indeed. Well, just off the top of my head, I'm thinking that whether true or not, *you* seem to believe it yourself, so that's something. I imagine you've been thinking about telling me this for some time?"

"Since the night I met you at Mark's."

"Right."

"You can see all the reasons I wouldn't."

"Oh, yeah. I see." He scratched his chin. "Just don't see what would have changed about all those reasons. But that doesn't matter as much as—"

"You finding out if what I say is true, and not some delusion of mine."

He smirked and bowed a nod.

"A demonstration," I said.

Another nod.

I had plotted out the conversation and how I would answer any subsequent questions, but for some reason never worked out how I would demonstrate.

I stood. Stan crossed his arms. I said, "Let me think ... Again, I've never done this before."

Stan took a step back and pointed a thumb at his chest. "Wait, you're not going to ... ."

"Oh no, of course not. I would never, and ... and that wouldn't show you anything besides." I walked to a window and peered down to the street, four stories below. A few people strolled the sidewalks. "I got it." I opened the window and sat back down on his couch.

Stan's dubious eyes held steady. I closed my eyes and left my body. Stan's focus remained on Geoffrey Cuion as I went to the window sill and plummeted to the street, into the ground and sewer tunnels, then back up to street level.

A moment later, Stan heard a voice from the street.

"Stan! Down here!" I saw his head pop out the window and gawk at the Puerto Rican man waving from the sidewalk. "It's Geoff!"

Stan glanced back into his apartment, then disappeared back inside. I guessed he was checking out my body, and, though I trusted him, I suddenly became dreadfully nervous about it being alone with him. I left the man on the street—he shook his head, peered around, and continued on his way—and I went back inside Stan's building, up the stairs to his floor. Passing through his apartment door, I found him back at the window, calling out.

"Geoff?"

"I'm here. I'm back." Stan flinched a little. I rose to my feet.

He chewed his cheek and stared at me, pensive. The sounds of the city filled the air as we remained silent for a time. Finally, a smile slowly spread into his cheeks and he stepped to his lounge chair, dropping into it with a swish.

"So you got a story to tell me now?"

We sat for hours as I recounted my life story. Each life I shared felt like a mountain had been taken off my chest. I fought through my fear of judgment as I detailed those minds I had inadvertently wiped, the ones I left with years of lost time, and then the wiping of Tinker. To my great relief, Stan did not judge. He saw my point of view, agreed with my every decision, including Tinker.

"Sounds like he was a real piece of shit. No loss to the world."

I wanted to draw the comparison between my action and a police officer executing a suspect on the spot because they appeared to be a scoundrel, but why push my luck? Stan was firmly on my side and that's what I had hoped. He didn't suspect me of having any involvement with his wife, he didn't look at me differently, and he appeared fascinated by the possibilities my existence brought to bear. It seemed to reinforce his faith in God and an afterlife.

He paced behind the sofa, one hand on his hip, the other spinning in front of him as he asked me if I knew of any others like me, could I ever die, what other special powers I had.

I smiled and sighed at my own revelation, "You now know as much as me."

"I highly doubt that," he smirked. "You don't have work tomorrow. Tell me more. Spend the night. We'll get doughnuts for breakfast."

I blinked and swallowed and was struck by a sudden flash from my time as Jerome Johns: my friend and mentor, Quincy Holbrook, smiling, with a backdrop of the snowcapped Rocky Mountains. I wouldn't spend the night. I couldn't.

Michael Siemsen

4. Jerome Johns

Greeley, Colorado - 1951

After World War II ended, everyone was afraid there wouldn't be enough jobs in the country. Having filled the labor vacuum for years, many women had no interest in being relegated back to housewives, and hundreds of thousands of soldiers needed work. Whispers and shouts of another post-war Great Depression dominated most conversations.

I had decided that I would not be one of those at the bottom this time around. I would take the body of someone at little risk of destitution. After a few days of searching, followed by a few more of studying, I settled on Jerome Johns, the son of an affluent businessman in Colorado. His father, Jack Johns, owned several repair shops for automobiles and farming equipment. Since I knew a fair amount about auto mechanics, I felt comfortable sliding into such a family.

The Johns family was not as close as I had initially thought, but at the time, I still wasn't particularly keen on joining someone else's family. I wanted to be my own man, independent and secure, and from what I could tell, that's exactly what would be expected of me as Jerome.

Jack Johns was a self-made man. He grew up in a poor farming family in Oklahoma and had been able to break out of poverty with his inventive mind and strong business sense. However, a couple decades later, this meant that his three children would not be sucking on any silver spoons. Jerome, his brother, Nick, and sister, Nancy, would have to work hard and make their own way. I later learned that as the children grew up, Mr. Johns frequently reminded them that they would each inherit a great fortune, but "… until that day, you won't be getting shit from me." When this came to my attention, I didn't mind so much. I wasn't afraid of hard work.

Twenty-three-year-old Jerome worked at his father's biggest repair shop, a sprawling hangar and warehouse complex where combine harvesters and other large farming machines were repaired. He was tall, handsome, fit, and muscular. He had been recently caught cheating on his fiancée, and so the wedding had been called off. This was good for me. I wouldn't have taken him if he was in the middle of a relationship. Women notice subtle changes better than anyone else, particularly in their boyfriends or husbands, for obvious reasons.

Jerome seemed to know a good deal about the combines and so I borrowed Tucker, one of the newer mechanics, for a couple weeks to learn the ins and outs of the shop, people's names, and his family dynamics before I would step into the role of Jerome. Folks seemed to seek Jerome's help frequently and I couldn't have him suddenly become incompetent. This foresight worked out well for me, and when I finally did become Jerome, no one seemed to bat an eye. Well, Tucker was a little confused, but that was due to the stinging knock I gave his skull to explain his memory loss. Everyone else spoke to me as if nothing had changed, and went about their affairs. Except for one man named Quincy Holbrook.

Quincy worked in the business office at the shop, buying the parts and other supplies we needed from our vendors. He was of average height and build, if a bit round, and always seemed to be either annoyed or pensive—rarely anything else. During my first couple months as Jerome, I dealt with Quincy a few times a week, submitting orders, brief hellos and goodbyes, and otherwise limited interactions. One time I overheard him speaking with Trudy, the accountant, in the lunch room.

She didn't know I was in the room and she was complaining about some of the mechanics. With Trudy's eyes focused on her cup of coffee, Quincy peered up at me and grinned as he let her go on.

"Not a single one of them knows the first thing about arithmetic, but they want me to explain how this adds up to that, or why the number at the bottom of their check doesn't seem to add up to what they thought." She looked up at Quincy's face and his expression quickly shifted to an empathizing frown.

He nodded. "Outrageous." She didn't catch his sarcasm.

"Pay them in cash, though, and their eyes go all googly. Idiots, every one of them." She turned her attention to her sandwich and he gazed back at up me with a deviant smirk. I smiled back and slipped out before Trudy noticed me.

Later that week, Quincy strolled up to me outside the hangar as I tightened the chain on my Indian motorcycle.

"How about that weather, huh?" he said. I glanced up. He had his hands in his pockets and was peering off in the distance at the mountains.

I wasn't sure if high 70s in September was irregular, so simply replied, "Yeah, it's been nice."

He lingered, "Mm-hm, awful nice ... Wonder if it'll rain soon."

I shrugged.

I stood up when I was done and wiped the grease from my hands on a rag. Quincy was still staring off at the mountains. "You need to talk to me about something, Quincy?"

"Huh? Oh, not really, no."

I climbed on my bike and said an awkward good-bye, riding back to my little house in a remote corner of the expansive Johns ranch.

A couple weeks later I figured out what the odd encounter was all about. It was a sort of Quincy test to see if I'd engage in small talk. Quincy and I had arrived to work at the same time and parked near each other. We walked together to the office entrance.

"Brisk morning, eh?" he said. There was a strange mocking tone to his voice.

"Yep, a bit chilly," I replied.

"How 'bout them Dodgers, eh?" He still sounded odd to me, as if hinting at a particular response.

I stopped walking and we turned to each other. His face appeared expectant.

Studying his expression, I asked, "Quincy, is there something else you wanted to talk about?"

"Not a big sports fan, are you?"

"No, well, not that. It just seems like you're trying to get at something. Is it just me, or did you really want to discuss baseball?"

"I'd rather be crucified," he said flatly.

I smiled, surprised. "Okay, so what is it? Tell me."

"You're not like the rest of *them*," he said, thumbing the hangar toward the shop area. "I always thought you were, but I've been thinking I was wrong."

Interesting…

"Is that a good thing? In what way?"

He brushed off my question and gestured for us to continue into the office. "You read at all, Jerry? Can I call you Jerry?"

"Sure, Jerry's fine. Read, as in the paper? Or do you mean books?"

"Come see me before closing and I'll give you something."

I was still working on a seized tractor engine with a couple of the other guys when closing time came around. Quincy strolled up to us, nodded hello, and signaled for me to follow him outside. We walked to his truck where he pulled a book from behind his seat. I looked at the title.

Being and Nothingness by Jean-Paul Satre. *An Essay on Phenomenological Ontology.*

"Phenomen—" I attempted. "Phenonemelog—"

"Phenomenological," he said. "But don't be intimidated. Just give it a shot, take your time, and let me know what you think." He patted me on the back and climbed in his truck.

I started the book that night, admittedly struggling at first. I had to consult my dictionary several times per page, but after a couple of chapters, I began to *get it*. I *got it* at a level beyond anything I had previously understood. Moreover, I found myself *thinking* at a level I didn't know existed—a higher plane of thought, I supposed. The phrase, "he opened my mind" is a perfect description of what this book had done for me. What Quincy had done.

The next day at work, my face must have betrayed my thrill. Quincy had nodded knowingly. "You're welcome," he said with a smirk. "Keep reading and let's get together this weekend. If you're not busy ... ."

That weekend was amazing. I probably spoke and listened more in those two days than I had in the months since I'd become Jerome. How refreshing it was to engage with another man that had more on his mind than "skirts" and "wheels." We discussed consciousness, self-deception, perception, and Sartre's other theories. The following weekend was more of the same, and the weekend after that. Quincy and I became the best of friends. He inundated me with books, always invigorated whenever I came to grasp one of these volumes he'd so long treasured.

We would also borrow horses from my (Jerome's) father and go out camping in the mountains. Connecting with nature, Quincy believed, was what humans needed even more than connecting with other people.

* * *

Four years passed, and our friendship only solidified. People in town would joke and say things like "Where's your husband?" or "Separated from your Siamese twin today, eh?" because we were always together. Our names were always spoken as a pair: "Quincy and Jerry" or "Quince and Jer."

Girls flirted with me here and there, or tried to get me to ask them out, but I was seldom interested. There were a couple, yes, that I spent some time with. I even *technically* lost my virginity to a persistent second cousin during a dreadfully awkward encounter in a reeking basement. A family of raccoons had watched. But I eventually found most local girls to be shallow or vapid, and moved on.

In the early spring of 1955, Quincy and I planned to go out backpacking into the Rockies. While we were gathering food and supplies in town, we were talking about Eliphas Levi, the 19th Century occult author. The night before I had been reading one of his books, finding myself deeply enthralled by a particular passage:

> *...thus this mortal's belief that the material universe is only a small part of total reality—the reality beyond humanity's limited ability to observe—which includes many other planes and modes of consciousness. If one wishes to achieve full knowledge and full power in the universe, said can only be attained through acute awareness of these other aspects of reality... the principal aspect being the **astral light**, a pliable cosmic fluid which by will may be molded into physical forms.*

I wondered, *Am I astral light? Did Levi possess some firsthand knowledge of my kind?*

As we walked the sidewalk from the sport shop to the grocer, Quincy lost his footing in a tree planter and crumpled onto his legs. He clutched his ankle and rocked as he winced.

"Damn clumsy feet," he murmured.

I crouched and looked, my hand on his shoulder. "Is it twisted?"

"Not sure," he said as he slid his sock down to expose the ankle. "Only one way to find out. Help me up."

I slung his arm over my neck and we got him up on his good leg. I held him up his arm and held tight around his waist as he tested putting weight on the bad ankle.

"What's the verdict?"

He pressed a little harder on the foot and bobbed his head. "I don't know. Definitely not broken, but not sure I can put ten miles on it tomorrow. Let's get our food anyway and see if ice doesn't help out back at the ranch."

We walked the rest of the way to the store in the same tight embrace, as Quincy limped along.

I laughed. "You know this will only bolster the Siamese twin thing."

Instead of laughing, though, Quincy turned to me, his face only a few inches from mine. "That doesn't bother you, does it? The twin thing ... The 'lovers' remarks?"

"What? No, of no, of course not. Let them talk, right? I was just joking ... ."

Quincy was pensive after that, but I didn't think much of it. He was always pensive. And he had always harbored negative feelings about those who lived their lives based upon what they felt others wanted, or clung to what society considered norms.

Back at the ranch we iced his ankle for a while and decided to see how he felt the next day. In the morning, the swelling had disappeared and there was no discoloration.

"I think it'll be fine, but let's bring something to wrap it with just in case. No way you're carrying me out of those hills if it goes south on me."

We rode our motorcycles to the trailhead, geared up, and began our hike. Snow still sat on the ground in spots, and overnight temperatures were expected to dip into the teens. We spent the first night in a small ravine by a river, opting to brave the cold and sleep outside under the stars. In the morning, both of us were freezing in our frost-coated sleeping bags. It had seemed a good idea at the time.

On the second night, a couple thousand feet higher up the mountain, we set up our canvas tent near a small pond and warmed ourselves by a fire, chatting about a new philosophy book we always said we would one day write. At one point, Quincy pulled a little box from his backpack and put it under my nose. I knew that it was marijuana.

"Are you going to smoke that?" I asked.

"*We* are going to smoke this," he replied, and saw my apprehension. "It doesn't make you go crazy like they say. Don't worry about it."

I was genuinely surprised to learn that Quincy did such things, and was apprehensive about using it. But I did. It felt good at first—I was overly amused by things he or I would say, but soon the feeling in my head grew too intense and I desperately wished to escape it.

"You all right?" he asked. I saw his concerned expression in the light of the flicking fire.

"I don't know," I said. "I think I need to lie down."

I went into the tent and curled myself between the thick floor blanket and my sleeping bag. My head buzzed and I felt like the ground was tilting beneath me. Scattered thoughts pulsed through my mind. The ground's movement eased, the muddle in my head cleared, and, eventually, I fell asleep.

I awoke in a haze—that globby feeling where you're not sure if the world is a dream. Dizzy, I tried to orient myself to where I was and what I was feeling. All was black in the tent. I was cold, exposed, but a strange warmth drew my attention down *there*. Something bad was happening.

My pants and shorts were down at my thighs. Quincy's head was there, his slimy mouth wrapped tight around me. He was trying to pleasure me. I lurched away and swung my fist at his temple.

"What the hell are you doing?" I screamed, pulling up my pants. "You sick bastard! Are you sick?"

He tried to soothe. "Jerry ... I'm sorry, Jerry, I ... I thought we were—"

I blasted out of the tent and yelled back at the flapping door. "Is this why you made me do drugs? You just wanted to knock me out?"

I heard him inside the tent, quiet, weeping. "No ... I didn't ... I thought ... I thought you would wake up and we ... I don't know what I thought ... ."

I went around to the side of the tent where he was and kicked at the canvas, striking him in the side or back. He released a quick squawk.

I packed up my things, all but my tent and sleeping bag, and hiked out immediately, leaving him there. I just couldn't believe that he would ruin everything like that—and why now? After four years? Whatever strange ideas or desires he had, he should have kept them to himself. Why wasn't our friendship enough for him? It was selfish. It meant that satisfying his maligned hunger was more important than our relationship. I seethed for the entire hike back to my motorcycle.

* * *

I went to work that Monday hoping he wouldn't show up. I hoped he would just quit without a word. Go away. I avoided going into the office or common areas. I worried that he must be there since no one came and asked me where he was. Everyone knew we were always together. Now they would notice a difference and ask what happened. What the hell would I say to that?

I was sitting in the driver's seat of a combine harvester we were working on, Tucker down in front loosening the thresher barrel. My mind was elsewhere.

"Fire her up!" Tucker yelled, and I started the motor. "All right, hang on a minute! Don't do anything!" He disappeared down below the guard.

I glanced across the hangar to the office door, wondering again if Quincy had decided to show up after all. What would I do if I saw him? I was still so angry—furious—but I didn't want to hit him again or anything. I just wanted him to disappear. I wanted to burn every book he'd given me, as if those too had been sullied like our friendship.

Tucker called out from below and I went ahead and engaged the thresher for him to test.

The office door opened and someone came out. I thought for a second that it was Quincy, but it was my father, Jack. He was looking right at me, waving. I waved back, wondering what he wanted. Then my hand began to feel the vibration of the stick, the muffled hum of the engine, and I realized that I hadn't been hearing anything. Sound returned to my ears, blaring and ghastly. Something had happened.

I shut down the combine and looked around. My guys were running toward me, office folks streaming from the door. A pair of hands launched up from beside me and I turned just in time to see my father grab me by the jacket and heave me from the seat. I slammed down onto the ground, watched his twisted face screaming at me. What had happened?

When I got up and slowly joined the throng of onlookers in front of the combine, their faces half-covered by their hands and arms, warped and horrorstruck, I finally realized what must have happened. And then I turned to the thresher and saw it for myself. Tucker was dead, his legs and one battered arm dangling like a scarecrow from the threshing drum. Blood coated everything around him.

I felt like I was floating. Surreal. My neck moved on its own, turning my head to search around for some explanation, but I found only expressions of disgust and hatred. Shouting and demands. Pushing and shoving. And then I saw the office door across the hangar, held half-open. Quincy stood there, peering out. He looked shattered and apologetic, devastated. We made eye contact. His hand went up to cover his mouth before he slipped back into the office and the door shut behind him. It's an image that has stuck with me, somehow moreso than the reddened combine. Quincy's face and all that spun behind it.

That night, I did the only right thing I could for Jerome Johns. I drove his motorcycle at 90mph down the highway, veering off the road into the side of an old condemned brick building. I robbed him of his life, just as I had taken Tucker's. I simply couldn't return Jerome to that sort of life—utter shambles, hated. The bike exploded and Jerome was killed instantly as I flew for several miles, my momentum sending me in a slight arc through brick, wood, the air, a sign, shrubs. I let myself continue on, passing deep beneath the earth until eventually stopping somewhere underground. I remained there in the pitch black, a self-imprisonment, cut off from the world, sights, sounds. I tried to solidify myself the way I would to stay in a car. I thought maybe that was the secret to ending my own life, but it didn't work. It just pushed me around a few inches.

I lost all sense of time. In the absence of other input, I was sequestered with only my thoughts and ever-looping images of all that had happened. It became so unbearable, and my outlook so devastated, that I believed that I had to remain there forever—that this was how I was to suffer. That *I* had gotten off easy with this mere mental torture. Tucker couldn't say the same. Tucker would never get to be sad again. He was no more. Or was he?

If I lived on after Grant Beauchamp hit Samuel on his bike, perhaps Tucker was now like me? Confused, but still around. Or maybe he went where I should have gone—the afterlife where I wished I had gone. Maybe Tucker actually had it *easier* than me. Or maybe I was merely exhausted with suffering, and this was my subconscious mind trying to make me feel better. Well, if so, it was working. I remained underground a little while longer and then slowly began my ascent. When I emerged it was nighttime, but I had no idea how long had passed. Perhaps just the day? Surely no more than two days.

I found my way back to the highway and followed it to a gas station. I borrowed the body of a truck driver, drove back to the Johns ranch, and sneaked into Jerome's house. I grabbed my things: cash, my knife, keepsakes from other lives I kept in a box in the closet. I was about to leave and took a final glance around the room. The bookshelf caught my eye, the spine of Being and Nothingness standing out among the rest.

Bring them or leave them...?

I finally decided to gather some of my favorites with the rationale that I would need them to get through a very difficult time. I may have gotten them from Quincy, and I may forever associate their contents with him, but it wasn't as though he *wrote* the books. I couldn't let what happened damage my appreciation for the wisdom of the ages. That would have been a further tragedy.

I would set things right in my next life, I determined. I would do things better. And above all, I wouldn't put myself in a situation where other people's safety was in my hands.

5. Eileen – Part One

Bronx, New York - 1959

Often, one can only appreciate the gravity of an event when looking upon it in retrospect. In my memory there seems to be more than a hundred occasions of this sort—incidents, introductions, decisions—but none so significant as meeting Eileen. In reality, my introduction to Stan was the true beginning of this chain of events, but that only became evident later. Retrospect.

I slouched into a reclined posture and read the newspaper in the rear car of the Lexington line, on my way to Stan's in the Bronx. Each Monday the two of us got together and watched *Tales of Wells Fargo* and *Peter Gunn,* with E-Z Pop popcorn.

My view of the aisle obscured, I vaguely heard the *click-clack* of approaching heels, but was much more enthralled by the front page articles. The Soviets had launched a rocket that had just passed the moon on its way to orbit the sun, and Alaska became the forty-ninth state.

Forty-nine states, I recall thinking. *That's going to be a tough one to get used to.* My last thought before I knew she existed—my undistracted mind devoted to one of the endless trivialities I could think about before *her....*

"You don't look the type," said a woman's voice nearby.

I bent the paper toward me and peered around to see if the voice had addressed me or some other. One seat up and across the aisle sat a breathtakingly beautiful woman. She wore a black satin hat with netting draped to her nose, striking red lipstick, and a form-fitting camelhair coat. Her face was pale and perky with soft features I was certain I had seen in movies or television.

I tended to avoid women at that period in my existence. In my mind, I had so many other interests, and of higher priority, than women. To date, my experiences with the opposite sex had always left me feeling inadequate, bumbling, unprepared. Sure, I thought about them and would steal the occasional glance, and I was reasonably certain that the desires I felt were normal. But I did not pursue. It just wasn't in me. This inaction, I realized, would not get me any closer to fulfilling my deep yearning for love and family. But a mate would just swallow up my life, and there was so much to be done!

In reality, other interests and priorities were an excuse. In truth, I was afraid. Even the most timid of women seemed to hold an overwhelming power. The mere idea of striking up a conversation would send panic into my belly, and regardless of whether I'd recently handled it, a violent bowel movement would frequently come banging on the back door. It was as though I had some secondary set of bowels always on call should a woman hold eye contact too long, or worse, *speak* to me.

This woman on the train was doing both.

I suddenly found myself in desperate need of water and unable to swallow. I crushed the newspaper into a ball with one noisy motion, grasped the seat back in front of me, my eyes surely bulging as I attempted to appear calm and casual, all while unable to breathe. She simply smiled and waited with perfect eyebrows hovering high on her forehead. I knew I looked like the greatest fool that ever was, the bumbling bookworm rendered stupid in the presence of a pretty lady or cross-dressing rabbit—I personified the caricature of lovestruck males from cartoons.

I finally choked out a response. "Beg pardon?"

"I said you don't look the type."

I nodded recognition; it was a brilliant observation. She was both beautiful and brilliant. But I didn't know what she was talking about.

"Sorry." I was finally able to swallow, followed by my attempt to rapidly release every word that had queued in my head. "The type for what you're quite the handsome, by the way ... Sorry, I meant that as two. Two sentences. And not ... ." I sighed and gave up. Things were getting worse by the second and I could feel my belly brewing tragedy.

I shook my head, adjusted my glasses, nodded to her, and uncrushed my newspaper in front of me, creating a wall to hide behind.

"Is that all?" she said. "You give up? You might regret that later."

I pulled the paper aside again. "I think I'll regret it more if I continue attempting to speak. Good day to you, Miss."

She giggled. "See, you got that one out just fine." She stood and stepped back to my row, taking the seat beside me. *Directly* beside me, not across the aisle. I shimmied closer to the window to avoid our legs or elbows touching. Who knew what might happen if contact occurred? My back sweat began saturating my undershirt.

No use. She wrapped one hand around my wrist while the other slid my half-rolled sleeve farther up my arm, revealing in whole one of Tinker's most vile tattoos: a nude woman straddling a giant snake, back arched in ecstasy. I slapped my hand down over it.

"I'm sorry!" I said. "That is, you shouldn't have to see such things."

"Hmm. How gallant. Someone you know? She looks like a fun girl."

"Absolutely not! I would never—"

"A stranger then? Someone you saw and always wanted to have riding your snake?"

My face clamped shut. She tilted her head to me, waiting, the corners of her mouth curled ever so slightly. She was enjoying seeing me squirm. Fascination and surprise lit up her face. I realized, even before this moment, that me and Tinker didn't quite mix in the eyes of the ladies.

Once I had cleaned him up, Geoffrey Cuion was a conspicuously handsome man. His intense blue eyes, strong features, and physique always caught the attention of women. As a result, I tended to watch the ground and slouch. Not because I hated the attention, but for fear of their disappointment once they actually spoke with me. And this wasn't paranoia! I experienced it with some frequency: the initial intrigued look, the flipping of hair to catch my attention, the moving closer, the casual comment or question. And then, my response, followed by their confused look and occasionally polite escape.

Now, I do not hold myself in so low a regard as to truly consider my personality repulsive. I simply believe that the *type* of woman that found Geoffrey's appearance attractive was not the type that would say the same for *me*, Samuel.

And so I hunched, I hung my head low, kept my hands in my pockets. A few years in, I didn't have to worry so much about those disappointed faces. However, the reverse appeared true of this woman on the subway. She not only spotted the incongruence, she was captivated by it!

I had to go. It would be one stop early, but I could walk it without arriving late to Stan's. I folded my crumpled paper as neatly as I could and gestured that I needed to get up for my station.

"Oh, no," she purred. "And I *really* wanted to hear your story. There's something different about you. Special." She stood and stepped aside to let me pass.

"Some other time, perhaps." I walked to the doors and gripped the pole as the train slowed to a stop.

Click-clacks approached behind me.

"This is my stop, too," she said. "Whaddya know?"

"That's ridiculous. I mean coincidence. That's ... something."

She curled her hand into the crook of my arm. "We'll walk together until our paths diverge. I'm certain it'll be plenty of time for you to tell me what you're all about." She leaned close. I could feel her breath, smell her perfume, floral and exotic. "Because I am *extremely* curious."

We ascended the stairs to street level, her scrutinizing eyes visible in my peripheral. Dirty snow was piled in banks at the sides of the road, but the skies were clear. My adrenaline must have been pumping at full strength because I couldn't feel the brisk air on my nose or ears and my stomach pain had subsided.

She clutched my arm tighter, leaning in again. "So, are there more?" But before I could answer she began squeezing with both hands up the rest of my arm. "Hmm ... Some muscles in there, too." Her hands continued on to my chest, examining me like a doctor. I stopped walking and grabbed her wrists, facing her.

Titillated, she said, "Ooh. That's more like it."

"Listen, you are probably the most beautiful woman I've seen in this city, but I don't know what you want with me. I ... I don't think I'm who you think I am."

Her eyes had grown wide—thrilled—her teeth bared in a deviant grin. "And who *are* you pretending to be?"

What the heck does that mean? I wondered. Another example of me reading into certain phrases.

"I'm not pretending to be anybody. I'm ... I'm me."

"Are you?" She grabbed my arm and tried to pull the sleeve up again. "Tell me that again while I look at your naked lady fucking a snake. Is it symbolic of a giant cock? What do you got down there, anyway?" She reached to my crotch and squeezed through my trousers, feeling the erection I had been trying to hide. "Well, hello, Mr. Wilson!" An image of my mother popped into my head, the scent of her hair. I jumped back, unbearable chills scurrying out from my spine.

"I beg your pardon, Miss! I am not ... that is not the sort of behavior I would expect from a lady! If you don't mind, I believe we should part ways. Good evening." I continued up the block, squeezing my eyes shut, trying to banish my mother's visage from my mind.

She called after me, "What are you, some sort of queer?" I didn't look back. "Get your rocks off with little boys, do you?"

Passers-by recoiled and looked at me with disgust. I quickened my pace as the woman continued shouting after me.

I knocked on Stan's door, but he didn't answer. I could hear the television on, but no other sounds. I knocked again. "Stan?" Nothing. I fetched the spare key from atop a pipe in the laundry room down the hall, and let myself into the apartment. Stan was sprawled out on his couch, sleeping.

I nudged his shoulder. "Stan, wake up. You gotta hear what just happened." Nothing. He wasn't moving. Concerned, I looked at his chest and saw it rise and fall. "Stan!" I slapped his cheeks. Nothing.

I backed away from him, a horrifying thought occurring to me. What if the daimon that took his wife had finally come for him? I circled the couch, thinking, then returned to his side and knelt.

"Stan?" I slapped his cheeks again, this time harder. I began to panic. I brought my hand down on his chest with a strong slap and shouted. "Stan!"

His arms and legs flailed up as he gasped.

"Geoff! Good Lord! What's happening? Ow!" He winced and nursed his chest.

I exhaled and crumpled to the floor, the relief and residual terror dancing in my head with a thundering buzz.

"I'm sorry," I said. "I got scared. You were—"

"*Snoozing*, buddy! Long day. Was dreaming about a cartoon cloud with arms and legs ... wanted to pull me into it. So strange. What time is it?"

"Just past seven."

"Dang it! I didn't fix anything." He looked around, flustered. "Hey, I've got a TV Dinner in the freezer. You want it? Turkey."

I lied and told him I wasn't hungry. He got up, stretched, and went to the kitchen to fix the TV dinner for himself. As it cooked, I recounted my experience with the woman.

Stan listened, appearing mildly intrigued. "You think she was a hooker?"

"I don't think so. She was ... I don't know ... too pretty. I mean, she was perfect! Black hair in this great sort of updo, and well-dressed, too. But that mouth on her ... It didn't match at all."

"Sounds like a lady I've seen around my building. The looks, not the mouth, though we never really talked. Real stunner named Eileen. Sure doesn't give *me* the time of day. How tall was she?"

"About my height."

"That short, huh?" He smiled. "Just foolin'. Yeah, I'll bet you that's Eileen. Now that you mention it, she just *might* be the best looking broad I've seen in the city. Why didn't you ... ah ... ."

"I don't know!" I laughed. I knew it sounded ridiculous. Stan and I didn't really speak of women, what with losing his wife and all, but I didn't think he'd judge or think less of me for my incapacity. "I was just so ... intimidated. She was so forward. And then later, on the street, well, you can understand."

"Sure, sure. I meant on the train, before she turned into a sailor on you."

I shrugged. "If she hadn't come and sat next to me, maybe I would have ... I don't know. I'd like to think I would have asked her name and number. Maybe not, I don't know. This gal, so out of my league. I also didn't want to leave you in the lurch here, you know. We had our plans."

Stan dipped his chin at me. "God help ya, buddy. I'd much rather you get your dipstick checked by a hot little number than laze on a couch with me in front of the tube. I'll survive."

My stomach rumbled as we watched our programs. Stan finally made the popcorn before Peter Gunn came on and I devoured it.

*　*　*

At 9:30 I pulled on my coat and bid Stan goodnight, hoping I'd be able to find a hamburger somewhere between there and home. Halfway down the four flights of stairs I heard a slow, ominous rhythm: *click-clack click-clack*. I stopped and peered over the handrail. One-and-a-half stories down, there she was in her very same outfit from earlier, her hand sliding up the polished wood with a squeal. Panic set in once more. I contemplated darting down the third floor hall, but with my luck she would happen upon me, outraged, and start in again: "Are you fucking *hiding* from me, queer man?" I poked my head over the rail again to see if she would turn down the second floor hall. She curved around and continued upward: *click-clack click-clack*. No such luck. I stiffened, pulled up my coat collar, took a deep breath, and began down the stairs in a hurry. I hoped to fly right by her as if in a rush, passing without allowing her time for an upward glance.

I sped down the cement stairs, taking the outside course to avoid bumping into her, and timed our passage to occur at a landing. This would ensure the briefest contact.

Not quite. She heard me coming, stopped right before the landing and stared right at me when I appeared around the corner.

"You!" She said.

I shook my head, avoided eye contact, and maintained momentum. To me she was like some unknown, potentially vicious stray dog. If slowly backing away from her wouldn't have been even more embarrassing than our earlier interaction, I would have done it. She reached for my arm as I passed.

"Hey ... Mister ... ." she spoke softly, put a gentle hand on my shoulder. "I'm truly sorry about earlier. Truly, I am." I stopped and looked up at her face. It was earnest and repentant... beautiful again.

"It's all right. No hard feelings." I continued on.

"Well, hang on a second." She took one step down toward me. "You in a rush to get somewhere?"

"Kind of. I ... ah ... ."

"Look. Before you make up some place you gotta be so you can get away from me, let me just say something, and then I'll let you go if you still want. And no hard feelings, like you said." She pulled the netting up over her hat, exposing her full face.

I looked at her eyes and nodded for her to proceed.

"Listen, I'm not trying to sound egotistical, but I'm not used to men turning me down. I mean, I'm not usually the go'er after'er, if you know what I mean. I was genuinely intrigued by you, and when you didn't seem interested ... well, I guess I sort of cracked. That's never happened before. I am not some easy girl, I want you to know." I nodded, straining to maintain eye contact, battling the impulse to run. Why did I have to be so terrified? She went on, "But you, you're something different. You're special. You might have some crazy past, but the man you are now, believe it or not, I *see* you."

"You *see* me? How—"

She took another step down to me. I could smell her perfume again. "I do. Unless you really are queer, but I don't think that's the case." She nodded toward my groin.

"I'm not."

She smiled and sighed relief and put her hands in her coat pockets. "I'm glad. So, can I walk with you, or ... where are you heading? You don't live here."

"No, a friend of mine. I'm ... well, I'm going home, but I was going to try to find a bite first. Didn't eat dinner."

"Oh! I know that the burger place up the block is open another ... ." She glanced at her watch. "Twenty minutes. I'll show you the way if you'll let me. Hell, I'll buy you a fucking burger to make up for my earlier lunacy!"

It still didn't sound right to hear cursing like that from her, but I admit that halfway through her apology I was already feeling aroused. I wouldn't have thought there was anything she could say or do to turn me, but she had. And it wasn't just her beauty. Her attitude, her brazenness—despite rattling my nerves—was a real turn-on. Now, in all honesty, if she looked like she spoke, I wouldn't have given her a second thought. But she was *different.* Like she had said of me, there was something special about her. And not to be overlooked: she was strongly attracted to *me.* Interested in *me.* I'm not sure how many points that adds to a woman's appeal. Moreover, her earlier outburst and now this act of contrition—they seemed to put me in some position of power. *I* determined if she could walk with me. *I* could choose to accept her apology or not. It worked wonders on my confidence.

We walked up the chilly street toward the fluorescent glow of the burger joint. She kept her hands in her pockets, and so did I.

"So were you in the service?" She asked.

"No."

"Truck driver?"

"No."

"Docks?"

"No, I work at a library."

She snickered. "Sorry. Honestly?"

"Yes, the Aguilar in East Harlem."

"Huh. Well, all right. But before that ... I mean—"

"The tattoos ... You're wondering—"

"Christ, yes!" She laughed. It was a wonderful, vibrant laugh—infectious. I laughed with her.

"Where I'm from ... I was with this group of motorcycle enthusiasts."

"A biker gang? Wow, I'm impressed. Is that where you got that ghastly scar, too?" I ran my finger down my jaw. "Sorry, am I asking too much? I know we just met. You don't have to answer."

We continued walking in silence.

She went on, "Wait, you're really not going to answer? I was just being polite. You *do* have to answer." She poked me in the side.

I looked at her face: that devilish grin, those clever eyes. It was getting difficult to walk again. I hoped she would keep her hands to herself, but I also hoped she wouldn't.

"Yeah," I said. "It's a long story."

That appeared to further electrify her. "Oh, Mister ... Wait, you have to tell me your name. Let me say it aloud; see how it sounds screamed out in the dark. Or the light ... ."

I sighed.

"Sorry. Shit, I keep having to apologize with you! I'm not normally like this, you know? I want you to know that. You make me crazy. And I'm only joking. You get that I'm joking, right? My jokes get me in trouble sometimes. Am I talking too much? Should I shut up?"

We arrived at the hamburger joint. The window was still open, but I could see two people inside cleaning up the counters and griddle. I turned to the woman.

"My name is Geoff." I smiled and held out my hand to shake.

She sneered. "Geoff? *Geoff.* Geoffrey. Hrmf. You got a middle name? Only joking. Geoffrey's not bad. I'm Eileen. Eileen Scoville. *So* pleased to have met you." She gave me her hand and dipped into a little curtsy. I began shaking her hand but she lifted it to my mouth for me to kiss it. I took the cue and inhaled the smell from her wrist. Her scent was enchanting. She pulled her hand away. "Only joking. Let's get you some food. I felt that spare tire. Bet you're famished. Just joking."

My hamburger was begrudgingly prepared on a freshly cleaned griddle and I ate it outside on a concrete table. The inside dining area was closed. Eileen sat across from me, watching with her chin cradled in her hands, nibbling at the occasional French fry and sucking cola from my cup. It felt childish, but I was charmed by her nonchalant usage of my straw, her lips wrapped right over the spot where my lips had been.

Her questions and comments flowed like a steady breeze.

"Do you have a girlfriend? Do you work tomorrow? Do you think I look like Audrey Hepburn? People say I look like Audrey Hepburn. Why are you shy? Have you ever had a girlfriend? Have you ever killed someone? Too many questions? I love your eyes."

My answers were short, one- to-three word responses between bites. When finished, I disposed of my garbage and we stood looking at each other, the temperature surely dropping into the twenties.

"I'm freezing," she said. "What now?"

"Well, I don't know ... I—"

"Sorry, I don't know why I asked that. As if you'd have the gumption to say what you want, right? I'll make it easy for you, and I won't use any of the naughty words that make your eye twitch. I want to spend the *night* with you. We can go to my apartment down the block, or all the way to yours, but that would be extremely inconvenient for me. What do you say?"

I tried to appear confident and self-assured, but thirty minutes with Eileen did not render her any less intimidating. I stammered, "I ... Yes. I would."

"You would what? Which? Mine or yours? Mine, yes? Please say mine."

"Yes, there. Yours. Please."

"You're adorable." She took my hand and pulled me back down the street. "I'm going to figure you out, Geoffrey."

Her apartment smelled like a full bottle of her perfume had shattered on the floor. The living room was adorned with numerous skin rugs and furry throws. Zebra stripes at the entry, leopard print beneath the coffee table, a white rabbit blanket draped over the red leather sofa.

"I'm going to freshen up, all right? Don't run away on me. Only joking."

I gargled in the sink and looked around for any kind of mint or candy to mask my food breath. There were none to be found, but I did happen upon an interesting framed photo on the wall. Audrey Hepburn as *Sabrina*. There was certainly a resemblance, but ... .

"Her neck is too long, no? Too thin?" I turned and found Eileen looking up at me.

Without her heels she was a couple inches shorter than me. I peered down and saw she wore black lingerie, separated into two parts, exposing her creamy white midsection. But I didn't get to look for long as she pushed herself against me.

"Are you ready?" she asked, her eyes on my mouth. "I want to take all this off of you. May I?"

I nodded. She began to unbutton my shirt.

"You're not going to say a word for the rest of the night, are you?" She grinned.

"I can talk."

"Mm-hmm. Well done. Unfasten your belt." I complied. "Take off your shoes. Do your feet smell? I can't stand smelly feet."

"I don't—"

"Only joking. Come."

She led me into the bedroom, lace-lined pillows strewn all over the floor. The silken red bedspread was all that remained on the bed. I took off my glasses and she pulled my shirt all the way off, revealing my chest and shoulder tattoos. I tried my best to suck in my paunch.

"Oh my, yes. I knew it!" Her eyes tried to survey all of my torso and arms at once. "Look at this! What's 'MC'? Is that for motorcycle?"

"Yes."

"Road Devils, huh? Another naked lady. Aren't you the naughty one ... These hurt?"

"Not really." *Not me, anyway.*

She turned me around, examining the rest of my skin. I closed my eyes as I felt her soft fingertips glide down my belly, around my waist to my back, and then both hands converged at my right shoulder. This was the tattoo for which I was most ashamed. I thought even Eileen might be offended by it. If I had had the courage, I would have scraped it off with a straight razor.

"Jesus, Geoffrey. You pick this one out yourself?"

A welcome invitation for a fast-formulated lie.

"It was a terrible prank by other motorcycle enthusiasts. And I was thoroughly inebriated. I wish I could erase it."

She ran her fingers over it. "I like how you say that ... 'motorcycle enthusiasts,' hahah. Golly. Well, I like it! Though I don't know if that's physically possible. Or practical. Are there any more?"

"No, that's all of them."

"I hope you're not offended if I don't take your word on that. I'll need to inspect every inch of you. Is that okay with you?"

"Yes."

She reached around me from behind and unbuttoned my trousers, letting them fall to my ankles. Her hands explored the backs of my legs, tickling and even more arousing.

"No shortage of hair, eh Geoffrey? Very manly." She remained on her knees and turned me slowly around. "Christ was fucked, Geoffrey! You can put an eye out with that beast! That's it."

She yanked my shorts down and grabbed hold of me—too tight—I jumped.

"That hurt?"

I nodded.

"You like pain?"

I shook my head.

"Sorry. I do. Here, *make* me do it." She put my hands over her ears and let her arms fall limp at her sides.

I wasn't comfortable with what she wanted, but my brain was a dizzy blur.

"If you're as blind as you look right now, you're gonna wanna put those glasses back on."

I would do anything she asked, and I did, and I was rewarded for complying with her demands. Shortly thereafter she shoved me back onto the bed, flinging off her brassiere and hurriedly removing the rest of her lingerie. She didn't seem to mind the lights remaining on—in fact, I think she enjoyed it. Her body was flawless and she knew it. She climbed on the bed and straddled me.

"See what you do to me, Geoffrey? I'm dripping wet. Oh ... there goes your twitchy eye." Her deviant smile returned. "You don't like dirty things coming out of my mouth ... but you don't seem to mind sticking dirty things in it. Twitch twitch. I'm going to fuck you like you've never been fucked before." She froze, her face wary. "You've fucked before, right?" I nodded. "Well, not like this," she leered.

She was right. I had only made love a few times prior to Eileen, and only twice did it work out. Eileen kept my hands pinned at my sides for much of the activity. Even in the throes of instinct-commanded thrusts and pulses, I never felt as if I had any choice in what was happening. And possibly worse, a belittling voice in my head continuously mocked and demanded to know what was wrong with me. Why couldn't I just enjoy this, fully? *Any* other man on the *planet* would be in heaven—no thoughts, no worries, no shame or doubt. They would be animals doing what animals do. They would take control, do better, do more, please her.

Notwithstanding my conflicted emotions, our actual lovemaking lasted a mere ten minutes, and the only reason I lasted that long was because half the time I was in incredible pain. On top of me, she had shifted into angles that my manhood was not meant to achieve while erect. She watched my face, saw me wince and try to adjust, but she had only grinned in return and pushed me back, pinching my nipple between her fingernails. I slapped her hand away out of reflex. My pain seemed to stimulate her. The hand slap had sent her into a frenzy. She wanted me to hurt her more, but I would not.

She was also very vocal, and my fear of neighbors hearing her moans and profane, often blasphemous, outcries lent themselves to my longevity. In the end, she sped up and thrashed about, hunching and twisting, her nails tearing deep into the flesh on my shoulders. The seemingly incongruent mixture of pain and pleasure sent me over the edge and the two of us collapsed like a pair of wet chamois thrown to the ground.

After a slew of expletives, she said, "I've never peaked like that before."

Embarrassingly, until that moment, I had not been aware that women "peaked." This was not a fact openly discussed.

I said the only thing that came to my mind. "Likewise."

She rolled toward me, turned me by the cheek, fixed her eyes on mine. "No, really! The intensity! We're doing this again."

"I don't think I can—"

"I don't mean *right now*, nosebleed. Right now you need to get your shit together and go home. I'll call you."

She sat up in the bed, leaning back on her arms, her breasts just sitting there, exposed. I don't know why that stood out to me, what with all that had just occurred. I suppose I expected women to want to cover right up after intercourse. Such had been my previous experiences. But her comfort in the nude was the least of the differences between her and my demure past lovers.

Eileen and I would see each other again repeatedly over the following two weeks, and though I had as many internal voices screaming at me to run as those begging to keep her happy, I gathered the courage and poor sense to ask if she would be my lady. She laughed at me.

We did become an item, though—my deep-rooted longing to be loved overpowering every blaring siren warning me that this woman was dangerous. Our relationship slowly matured into something ever-so-slightly beyond evenings and weekends of shocking sex acts. My apartment became our primary meeting place, though she only rarely spent the night.

There was one thing about her—obscured behind all of her most obvious repulsive character traits—that I couldn't put my finger on until much later: she reminded me of my mother, Geraldine. It was the reason my mother had popped into my head that first night I met Eileen—an unnerving, sickening muddle of emotions and memories that had no business sharing the foreground of my mind. They did not occupy the same space because the two of them looked the same, or even shared behaviors. It was where they sat in my memory of them, some categorization based upon those who left the deepest impression on me, they who brought me joy, pain, or a tormenting combination of the two.

6. Home

Anaheim, California - 1933

I attended Samuel's funeral with my family, skirting about the grassy hill to avoid any feet coming too close. Nearly one hundred people showed up, but according to some of the townsfolk I had overheard, many of the attendees did not even know Samuel. My death, and my stepfather's potential motives for it, was the most interesting event Anaheim had seen in years, and gossips were short of fresh material. I did not understand this at the time, but I do now, all too well.

That afternoon the house was quiet, as if no one had returned. There was only my mother, Geraldine, my sister, Esther, and our mother's sister, Aunt Josephine, there to run the house and farm while Geraldine mourned. Esther and Geraldine retired to their rooms while Aunt Josephine fixed a stew for supper.

I wandered the house in search of familiar items, anything that might strike a chord, fix my memory. A family portrait hung above an elaborate white mantle in the living room. The artist had painted Geraldine and a six- or seven-year-old Esther with pale, glowing faces, a dreamy sort of light illuminated the backdrops behind their heads. Like my mother with her hand on Esther's shoulder, Grant Beauchamp's opposite hand rested on Samuel's shoulder. No one smiled. I hoped Aunt Josephine would take the painting down before Geraldine saw it again.

Upstairs, I checked in on Geraldine, curled up in her four-poster bed with a knit blanket wrapped tight around her neck and face. Subdued moans marked her exhales. I hopped on the bed and watched her stricken face for a time. Though I still could not summon a memory of her or this place, I was overcome by the compulsion to soothe her. Her anguish was my anguish.

The room was painted white, from the hardwood floor to the molding-rich ceiling. A few days' worth of my mother's outfits lay strewn around the floor. I noticed a large, dark-stained armoire standing against one wall, its doors wide open and contents emptied haphazardly into baskets on the floor. Grant's clothes. They would need to be removed, like the painting, along with anything else that might remind my mother of her pain. But what of the surely ample evidence of Samuel's seventeen years in this home?

I examined Samuel's former bedroom while Esther lay on her neatly made bed, across from the disheveled heap in which Samuel once slept. Esther's glassy, unblinking eyes remained fixed upon the ceiling—her face expressionless, breathing slight. I couldn't tell if she suffered the same as our mother, or if perhaps it was all too much for her. Had the loss of her brother (not to mention her *father*) yet become *real* for her, or was she too young?

On a small table between Esther and Samuel's beds sat numerous little wood sculptures. Samuel had apparently enjoyed whittling. A half-husked corncob, a dog, a little girl (painted, even), an intricate rocking chair, several miniature cups. Curled shavings littered the hardwood floor beside his bed and around an empty wastebasket.

In his wardrobe hung assorted shirts and overalls. A hook held a straw hat. I studied each item in search of a memory—the slightest inkling of a flash of a remnant—but it seemed I could have been in any stranger's house, equally nostalgic about their possessions. There was simply nothing for me to recall. The specifics of Samuel died with him, leaving only his essential consciousness: me. I could learn everything about him, but I would never truly *be* him again. I began to wonder if I was ever him at all. It seemed obvious enough, first appearing at the scene of his death, but aside from my guesses, I did not truly know what I was, where I had come from, what would happen next, or how I knew the things I did know.

I grew increasingly uneasy. The sound of the house creaking ... How could I identify this sound? Esther, an intermittent source of sighs in the room ... How did I know those were sighs, that she was a girl, that there are males and females? Even in my panic at these racing thoughts, I wondered what was wrong with panic? Why did I fear it? What might happen? Why did I believe there must be some limit to the number of thoughts or questions shooting through my mind?

What's a mind? Do I have one?

Following the example of my family, I hopped into Samuel's bed and remained there until the anxiety subsided.

Shortly thereafter, while the sun still hung above the groves to the west, Esther sniffed the air, got up, and went downstairs. I followed. We found Aunt Josephine in the kitchen, loading more wood into a stove beneath a steaming pot. Josephine was a formidable-looking woman with big shoulders and a wide jaw, like a man, and she stomped more than walked. Not in an angry sort of way, just always with a purpose.

"What are you fixing?" Esther whispered.

Josephine wiped back a sweaty strand of her wavy hair and whispered back, "Pork stew. It's almost done. Be a dear and fetch some more wood, you don't mind?"

Esther nodded, hurried off with intense determination. Josephine stirred and tasted and chopped green onions. When Esther returned, she had a splintered bundle curled against her chest. Aunt Josephine helped her set the logs down in the rack.

"Thank you, dear. You fair well?"

Esther nodded, brushed bark from her chest and sleeves. She stared down at the log rack and whispered, "It's ... It's just us ... ." Her aunt did not respond, began stirring the pot with a long wooden spoon. Esther pondered a moment and whispered again. "How long are you staying, Aunt Josephine?"

Josephine turned around, smiled, and clutched Esther by the shoulders. "As long as needed, dear." Esther's frame relaxed. Josephine continued, "If it's a whole week, it's a whole week." She released her niece and returned to the counter.

Esther looked to the floor, swallowed deep. They had a business—the farm—and a household to run, and soon it would be only the two of them, mother and daughter, to handle it all.

* * *

I can jump higher than I initially thought. I discovered this fact while hovering above the hardwood floor of the dining room, watching Esther set the table with spoons and forks. The screen door in front hadn't been latched and had been slowly flapping open and closed. Suddenly I heard a scritching sound approaching. It was a chicken. It was skittering across the hardwood floor, directly at me. I backed up, then *leapt*, landing on the cherrywood hutch from which Esther began pulling plates. The chicken clicked to a stop below, looked up at me with one eye, then the other, then back to the first.

"What you doin' in here, Hillie?" Esther hushed, then shooed the chicken back out the front door, latching the screen shut.

The bird could see me, or somehow otherwise sense my presence.

I remained on the hutch while food was served. The vantage point was preferable to that of a chicken.

While the family pecked at their supper, a new sensation arose in me, a burgeoning panic. My *form*, I suppose I'll call it— which though invisible, feels to be the size of a melon or large grapefruit—began to spread or thin. It was painful; it felt as though I might evaporate and disappear. At the same time, the subtle waves emanating from the three women before me had become more pronounced, as if beckoning me to come inside. Esther, especially, boasted an enchanting glow. Long, blurry coils stretched out from every part of her body. Her ankle, exposed just below the hem of her dress, looked like something I should examine closer. Just take a quick look. Perhaps allowing her waves a brief caress would help to subdue my growing desolation ....

No. I would sooner allow myself to disappear—if that's what eventually happens—before ruining one of them. I would need to be strong—resist such temptations.

After supper came to a silent end, I moved periodically from room to room, sat with the grieving women, watched them toss and turn, stare into the darkness, cry. At some point while I hovered at the foot of Geraldine's bed, Esther tapped her nails on the door and crept in.

"Mama?" was all she said, and then slid into the bed, curling into her mother's back. While Geraldine did not turn or embrace her daughter, they both seemed to calm a little.

The opposite was true for me. I confined myself to the far corner of the bed for fear of being too near to resist their draw. But for as close as I lay to them, I was just as alone as ever. This feeling did not improve over the next few days, and my physical pain only increased. I knew I was starving for a body. I had to go.

I left in the morning of my sixth day of existence, heading up the road from the house. I paused for a moment at the spot where Mr. Beauchamp drove his truck into Samuel's bicycle. Winds had reset the disturbed dirt, leaving no sign that anything had ever happened there. I wondered what Mr. Beauchamp had planned after killing his stepson. Claim he hadn't seen him? Perhaps he was going to load the boy's body and bicycle into the truck and dispose of them somewhere no one would ever discover. Samuel had simply gone missing. This has afforded me some small comfort, knowing that my impulsive, aimless appropriation of Grant's body had been in many ways an inadvertent administration of justice. That Geraldine would not that night have been nestled beneath her blankets, her hair and shoulders caressed by her son's murderer.

I followed the road to its end, then the next, on and on through fields and plains, mindful of remaining on a consistent course. As night fell I longed for a warmth I'd never physically felt. I wished I was in a house, in a bed, near my family. Even though I had no memory of them, I believe there was still an emptiness where they should have been. When I was at the house, I felt like I belonged there. Perhaps I would have had the same feeling at some neighbor's house—I don't know. Maybe if I hadn't seen my body on the side of the road, watched my mother and my sister mourn, I would have had a different outlook. But I did ache to return to that house. There had been a sort of warmth in it that I cannot describe. It may have been simply *comfort*. Though had I *ever* really felt that, either? No, but certainly more so at the house than in the black wide open of wherever I'd ended up.

Looking behind me, I realized there was little chance I would be able to find my way back to the farm. Insects and frogs sang all around me—frantic, yet routine. There was another noise, an inconsistent low murmur breaking through the buzzing. I followed the sound, realizing as I moved closer that it was a medley of human voices. A scratchy voice, a bassy one, others.

A line of trees gave way to a creek and the flashing orange of a waning campfire. I crossed the stream and joined the group, pleased to be once more near the living.

"Knock his teeth in, I ought," a scraggly old man said. His clothes were in tatters, a gray beard, no shoes.

"Again with the teeth, Rainy," said a younger, bearded, deep-voiced man. His attire, too, had seen better days. "When you ever knock in anything, let alone a tooth? Bulls got food in their bellies and clubs and chains."

"And the law on their side!" A woman's voice from somewhere off in the dark.

I noticed there were several covered bodies laid out around the area. More grungy men, mothers with small children bundled close, a shabby dog licking a paw. Most were asleep, or making the attempt.

Between the two men at the fire sat two silent teenaged boys. I watched the boys' eyes dart from the fire to the old man, to the bearded man, and back to the fire.

"I can get a club." The old man labored to reach for a nearby branch. "Hell, I'll make one'a my own. 'Sides, they won't expect nothin' from an old codger like me. I'll knock their teeth in!"

The teenagers smirked and stifled their laughter. The bearded man made no such effort.

"Okay, Rainy. You take 'em all out for us and we'll all hop the next train in peace, forever in your debt."

"Don't tell 'em that," the unseen woman said. "They'll beat 'em to death, and ain't no law gonna raise a finger."

The site remained quiet for a few minutes, save for the crackle of the dying fire.

"Papa?" One of the boys broke the silence, addressing the bearded man. "I thought we was gonna go out lookin' for work here."

"*Were* gonna, son. *Were*. Don't talk like you don't know nothing. Wilbur said the farms here are miles out. Better to keep on south where the rail heads right through a big group'a farms all in one spot."

The other teenager looked up from the glowing embers, regarded the man. "But, sir, ain't that where everybody gonna go? Maybe them farmers ain't lookin' for no new folk on account'a they got so many 'bos comin' into town."

The man turned only his eyes to the boy, an unveiled look of disdain. "What you sayin', Rip? You think we ought'a pack up fifteen people and huck it twenty miles for perchance?"

The boy, *Rip*, shrunk. "Nah, I was just thinkin' ... ."

"Well, why don't you go take a hike? Go on. Go find you some work and come on back before the next train, and we'll pack it up and follow you."

Rip couldn't read the malice in the man's words, but somehow I could. He apparently wasn't liked by the man, and had no family among the group. But Rip had been right. If he found his way to the Beauchamp farm, they would most certainly pay him as a farmhand. Perhaps even board him. Geraldine, especially, might appreciate the presence of a boy Samuel's age.

Perhaps one could see where this is leading. Where it led. It wasn't my plan to begin with, but at sunrise, when Rip gathered his things—a sleeping bundle, some old cans, a few extra clothes—I followed the boy on his journey west into Anaheim. I listened as he whistled tunes and practiced impersonations of the old man, Rainy, and other voices I didn't know.

As sweat began to bead on his forehead, the unshaded noon sun blazing down for miles, Rip gulped down the last of his water. After a while he began broadcasting the same impressions for lengthy periods.

"I gots greenies on my toes! Greenies on m'toes! I gots greenies on my toes!"

We eventually reached town, and soon an intersection I recognized. We were near the police station. I knew the way back to the farm from this place. Rip found a pump behind a large cannery building, drank his fill of water, and refilled his cans. Back on the main road, he peered around in search of work prospects.

I didn't know what I was waiting for. Maybe I had hoped he would find his way directly to the farm and then I would have to make a decision. In reality, I was simply procrastinating—denying that I had already made up my mind to take him. Maybe I wished he would make a poor choice, head into a dangerous situation for which the only option for rescue required I take his body. In the end, I gave in to myself when he walked up the steps to the leatherworks shop.

I entered him and stopped with my hand on the door lever. He felt dizzy—*I* felt dizzy. And extremely hungry. The stomach burned. I supposed he must have been used to it. Suddenly the door handle yanked out of my hand and I fell back a few steps, though caught myself before truly falling.

"Help you, son?" A man in overalls stood gaping at me from the doorway. He looked me over. "You work for someone?"

"Oh, I ... . " Rip's voice felt different than Mr. Beauchamp's. I guessed it was the dry throat. It pinched a bit to speak. "I was just a little lost. I'm fine now, thank you."

I waved and walked back up the road toward the farm, glancing back to see if the man was still watching me. He was, though I couldn't tell if it was concern or suspicion beneath his eyebrows. I gave another quick wave and turned the corner out of his sight. I ran, as if at risk of being caught with a stolen body. I made my way through an endless grove of orange trees until I approached an unfamiliar road. I picked some oranges, tore them open and sucked out all the juice I could, swallowed every scrap of flesh. I was halfway done before realizing this was my first time eating or drinking in a body. The officers at the jail hadn't bothered to give Mr. Beauchamp anything the day or night I was there. The taste was amazing. *Taste* is amazing. A whole new sense!

An hour later, I was walking up that same dirt road to the farm, the one I thought I'd never see again. But this time I was walking with real legs in a real body that, aside from some lingering hunger, felt pretty good. It felt right to me. All the while I pushed away the thoughts of the kid that used to live here. I didn't even try to justify it to myself. I simply removed the guilt in favor of anticipation about rejoining my family. It would be like Samuel never died.

I dropped my bundle on the ground and ascended the steps, peering through the screen door to see if Geraldine or Esther were downstairs. The sun beat down on my neck and back. I saw my shadow cast across the hardwood floor.

"Holy Jesus on the cross!" Geraldine lay on the sofa in view of the door. She screamed, "Esther!" and recoiled into the farthest corner of the sofa.

Harried footfalls echoed from upstairs and Esther appeared at the top of the stairs. "Mama? What is it?" Then she saw me. She appeared at first mystified, taking slow steps down the stairs.

I said, "I'm sorry to trouble you, Misses. Don't mean to cause any fright. Just looking for work."

Both relaxed a little, though remained cautious as they approached the screen door. Geraldine shielded her eyes from the sun and I realized I must have initially only appeared in silhouette. Geraldine had thought the ghost of her son had come visiting. Apropos.

Geraldine gazed past me, saw my bundle, then looked up the drive.

"You alone, young man?"

"I am, ma'am, yes. I have no family. I'm just looking for work, like I said. I'll work hard ... do whatever you need."

She and Esther both regarded me for a beat.

"What's your name?" Esther asked.

I hadn't planned for this obvious question, and when posed, my first instinct was to say "Samuel" and perhaps make up a surname, though I only knew a few. I stammered, unsure if "Samuel" would work for or against me. Finally, without ever coming to a conclusion, I said, "Rip. I'm Rip."

Geraldine sighed, rested her knuckles on her hip. "Well ... pleased to meet you, Rip. You happened upon us at an opportune time. Someone tell you to come'a knocking over here?"

"No, ma'am, you're the first farm I've stopped at since leaving the rails."

"Well, I think we do need some help. My sister will be back here soon and she'll let you know the this'n'thats. For now, why don't you set yourself in the barn and we'll get you some water and such. You're hungry, I take it?"

"Yes, ma'am. Thank you, ma'am. And you, Miss."

Esther had the same dazed expression as she nodded to me.

* * *

I spent the next two days working from dawn to dusk. Cleaning chicken coops and pigpens, chopping wood, hauling hay, and doing pickups and deliveries in Mr. Beauchamp's grill-dented truck. There was little interaction with Esther or Geraldine; Aunt Josephine was my boss, and when I completed a task she had three more waiting. She was cold and curt with me, and on my third day waking in the barn, Aunt Josephine came to me.

"I'm leaving and won't be back for a few weeks. Everything I had you do, you keep on doing, on that schedule. You ever finish early, you check in with the Misses and ask for more. You're a hard enough worker. Never caught you tramping about, so you keep that up and you might have work until winter."

"Thank you, ma'am."

"And you keep on with *that*, too. Don't get too comfortable with my sister and niece. Too familiar. Even if they seem to warm up over time, don't go thinkin' you're a part of the family, hear? Surest way to lose employment."

"Yes, ma'am."

Josephine turned to go, and then stopped. "What was your name, young man?"

"Rip, ma'am."

"Right. Listen here, one more thing, Rip. The Misses lost her only son, Samuel, just about a week ago. He was about your age. Wonderful boy. It could be that ... well, losing a son ... ." She paused, looked at my eyes as she played with her fingernails. "You know, you just go with what she wants. Forget what I said. Mind your manners, of course! But if either or both of them offer hospitality, you accept it. Go with it, you hear?"

"Yes, ma'am."

"I'll see you around, Rip."

Aunt Josephine had somehow known what would happen. Hospitality was most certainly offered, increasingly so, over the following months.

I learned a lot about the world from people's conversations. Folks would frequently drive up that road, coming to pick up orders. Thinking of me as some outsider, nosey customers often pulled me aside when Geraldine and Esther were out of earshot.

"Hey, boy, any new word on Mr. Beauchamp? He still playing the fool?"

"Awfully sorry, Mister," I'd say. "I don't know anything about that."

Some would leer. "Ms. Beauchamp flip the sign yet?"

"Sign?"

"Open for business." A vile wink.

I played dumb. "But we *are* open for business, Mister. Esther took your order yesterday."

After all the whispered talk of Samuel and Grant Beauchamp simmered down, conversations shifted to other subjects. I learned that the country was in crisis—that there were millions like the group I'd found by the river, with no work and no way to earn money to pay for food or housing. It was called the Great Depression. But despite the strife affecting the majority, the Beauchamp family was in no danger of financial ruin. Business had suffered a bit, but Geraldine's savings and assets were plentiful, and people apparently still wanted fruits and nuts. Though Mr. Beauchamp's sensational trial ended with him being sent to a lunatic asylum, his accumulated wealth was added to hers as if he had perished.

Geraldine, or Ms. Geraldine, as she requested I call her, grew progressively more generous with me. At first, I was invited in for lunches. Soon after, instead of Esther bringing me a cool dinner plate in the barn, I was called to join them for dinners, as well.

My living quarters, too, found themselves upgraded every couple weeks thereafter. I went from the barn to the basement, basement to the attic, attic to the sewing room.

Geraldine had explained, "Best to have you on the same floor as us should anything happen."

She gave me a shotgun that had belonged to Mr. Frohler, Samuel's real father. In my free time, Esther and I would shoot up the decrepit farm equipment behind the barn, or hunt for gophers in the fields. Needless to say, I loved my life. I would have been just as happy remaining in the barn, sharing the occasional lunch with Esther on the house front steps, working every day. But as Aunt Josephine had predicted, my family would want Samuel back. The deep sadness that had aged Geraldine's face had seemed to reverse itself, Esther was chipper and playful, and doing well in school. On her fifteenth birthday, Geraldine baked a cake and the three of us stood around it and sang, Geraldine's left arm slung over Esther's shoulders, her right arm over mine. Family. This was the portrait we needed to hang in that empty space above the mantle.

In the beginning, my mother would often slip and call me Samuel, or at least hang a prolonged *S* in the air. She would close her eyes, grow upset, and sometimes angrily cast me away. It was as if my presence only served to remind her of who *wasn't* around. Even after seven months, she would still slip from time to time, but the anger had gone.

"Esther, where's Sam—ah, Rip?"

"I'm right here, Ms. Beauchamp."

"Ah, yes you are. Be a sweetie and take these old things out to the shed, would you?"

It wouldn't even faze her, as if the name no longer stung. I took this to mean that the names were interchangeable in her mind. Truly, that I might as well be her son. No more would Esther come to me in the fields and warn me not to come around the house for a while: "My mother is crying again, so, you know ... ." Instead, she'd amble out, prattle on about a boy at school, then tell me to hurry up and "come home. Mama doesn't care if you finish a little early." *Home. Mama.*

Everything was just fine.

When winter neared, Aunt Josephine came out for a week to help prepare the farm and teach me some seasonal tasks. The first day she seemed thrilled with my work, gratified to see I'd been set up in a real bed in the sewing room. The second day, she was back to cold and curt. Even a little nasty.

"Drop that hose and get in that barn!" she yelled from the porch as I drank water. "You aren't close to done, you!"

'You?'

I hadn't been "you" for months. Something had happened between her and my mother, but I didn't know what. I did what I was told the rest of the week, ensured I was respectful at all times, and kept quiet at dinners.

The day after Josephine left was a windy one. You could see it building all day, the crowns of the orange trees thrashing about like a giant green ocean. I had gathered the livestock, closed up the coops and the barn, and shuttered the house.

"I hate wind," Esther moaned as the three of us sat in front of the fire.

The house creaked and growled. Outside, the sounds of tumbling buckets and rattling basement doors. I recalled the period I'd lived in the barn and was thankful once more to be in the house.

My mother had been mostly quiet and pensive all day. Her eyes hung on a blank wall, the floor, nothing in particular, it seemed. Staring at the fire, she eventually stood up and went to the stairs without saying goodnight to either of us.

"Night, mama," Esther called behind her.

She received only an "Mm-hm" in response.

The pair of us sat side by side and stared into the fire, the waves of heat licking our cheeks and eyeballs until we both had to scoot back a little.

"She's still sore," Esther finally said. "About Aunt Jo."

"What happened?"

"Well," Esther turned to me, "Mama was just telling her to mind her business and such."

"About what?"

"I don't know. I mean, I know, but I don't know what she said exactly. But it was about ... um ... about me and you."

I turned and looked at her, her glassy eyes flashing with the fire. She had a little smirk. "What about me and you?"

"Such like, I'm getting older and whatnot and how we're always together and such, me and you."

I truly had no idea what she was talking about—why that would be a concern. We were brother and sister, after all.

"Weird." I looked back to the fire.

"I told Aunt Jo we ain't kissed yet or anything, but if you want—"

"What? You said what? Why would you ... ."

"She was asking!"

I was disturbed and shocked and moved away from her. "That ... Esther ... We're never gonna!" And I got up and I went to my room. I could hear her sniffle and begin to sob behind me.

Shortly after, as I lay in my bed staring at the lines of white-painted wood in the ceiling, I heard her finally go to bed. She crept past my door, paused a moment to listen, then continued on. I was terrified of what would happen next. I should have stayed in the barn. I should have listened to what Aunt Josephine had said first. Don't get too familiar. But how could I have known?

I hoped it would simply pass, never to be spoken of again. I couldn't have my mother worrying that this hobo boy she took in would one day try to marry her daughter. How exactly do I fill the role of her lost son with that sort of looming threat? She simply needed to know there was no risk of it happening. It would be just like one of Esther's unrequited crushes from school. They came and went all the time.

The wind outside continued to howl and batter the barn doors. I looked out at the bright white moon, casting a beam across my face and the floor. I rolled onto my other side. It appeared I wouldn't be getting much sleep that night. The floorboard outside the door sounded a deep creak and my door handle clicked. I sat up on my elbows to see a figure creep into my room.

Oh God, no.

I whispered, "Esther, I really need to sleep."

"Not Esther," my mother said. She stepped into the moonlight; her eyes were squinted and puffy. "I can't sleep with all the wind ... so tired. Would you mind staying in my room for a short while? It'll make me feel better."

She held out her hand and I took it. I didn't know why she chose me instead of Esther, like usual, but to me it meant that I was finally, truly Samuel again, and all my worries about this little Esther thing blew away with the wind. We entered her room, closed the door, and she pulled me to the bed.

"You go on that side," she whispered. "Beneath the sheets and all."

It was where she had Esther lay when comforting each other after the tragedy. I slid in, lay on my side, facing her as Esther had. She nestled into her side, facing away. She inhaled deep sighs, relaxing despite the trembling windows.

"Closer, dear," she said. "And put a hand on my back."

I complied and inhaled the scents of the bed. Clean and warm, it blended with my mother's unique smell, her hair soap. I shifted closer still, put my nose just an inch from her back—close enough to take it all in, while mindful she could send me away if I crossed a line and made her uncomfortable, reminding her too much of Samuel.

She reached back and pulled my hand onto her waist, kept her hand atop mine. Small contented sounds exhaled with her breath. I was in heaven.

After a few moments, she sent an arm back without turning the rest of her body and placed her hand on my hip, caressing softly. Soon she reached farther, around to my backside and pulled me closer, against her. She hummed and took in deeper breaths, pushed her behind harder against me, writhed a little. I began to feel strange, wrong. While I had thought that she would reject me if I moved too close, I was now the one desiring separation. I began to roll back, to turn the other way on the bed, but she reached back again, clutched my waist and shoved me against her once more. And then she slid her hand between us, made contact with my manhood and began to rub it in small circles. My breathing hastened, heartbeat grew rapid. I needed to leave right at that moment. It felt *wrong*—*I* felt wrong. She seemed only to grow more excited. The entirety of my delightful world was swiftly crumbling from the minute force of a gesture—a tiny area of physical contact. What unfathomable power for a gesture to possess.

I pushed myself away from her back, unwrapped her fingers from around me, and scooted off the bed.

"What are you doing?" She sat up.

"I ... I have to go to bed."

"It's all right. Just come back in. Everything is okay, whatever happens."

"I'm sorry," I said and opened the door, knowing this was the end of my family life.

"Rip!" she exclaimed in a whisper. "She's just a little girl ... You need a real woman!"

I closed the door behind me.

First Esther and now my mother, it had become clear that I had not refilled the empty space left by Samuel. I had stepped into a new spot, and I would have never imagined the consequences.

In my room, I lay on the bed and watched the diamond-shaped moonlight glide across the floor, bend in half at the baseboard, then climb the wall as a square until it disappeared near the top of the door. Soon, the room brightened and a sliver of sunlight appeared at the top of the door, growing into a square that inched down the wall. When it reached the door handle, I rose and packed up my things to leave. Esther cried—didn't understand. My mother, however, apparently appreciated my motives, whatever she believed them to be. She gave me as many of Samuel's old clothes as I could carry, a package of salted meat, leather water bag, and $208.00—all the cash she had in the house. They waved from the top of the front steps, Esther still weeping, my mother downcast, apologetic.

I carried on as Rip for a few years after that—like I mentioned earlier, riding the trains, taking work wherever I could. But that night in Cheyenne, Wyoming, stripped naked next to my friends, beaten by a well-fed boy my age, a boy with a father, well I just couldn't stand it anymore. I was going to stop this Aaron Fuller thug from beating on my friends and any other kids that came to ride the rails. And that's what happened. No more beatings.

That's *one* side of leaving Rip behind.

The other side—unavoidable and often haunting—is the fact that Rip was *no more.* He laid there glassy eyed near an idling train, his friends shaking him to wake him up. They assumed the young bull walking away had simply beaten Rip dead. When they saw Aaron glance back, they must have seen the remorse on my face because they appeared confused.

Absent the invasion of an inexperienced daimon like myself, Rip would have continued with a harsh life—most certainly—but this fact has never eased my guilt. For all intents and purposes, I murdered Rip the moment I had taken him back in Anaheim.

7. Eileen – Part Two

East Harlem, New York – 1960

It's difficult for me to discuss Eileen without sounding weak and pathetic. I wish that I could rewrite history, exchanging the man I was at that time with the one I am now—make different decisions, reverse answers, and replace every instance where I remained silent or passive with a perfectly phrased statement. But none of that would have made a bit of difference. I know that now, though I still look back on the period as if alternate choices would have led to better outcomes.

In reality, I remained driven by the same goal that had always motivated me: to be seen, accepted, loved. It sounds melodramatic to me now, but I would be a fool to deny its continuing presence. Was I like this before I was ejected from my body? Was Samuel Beauchamp a desperate person? Or did my early daimonic experiences leave this indelible mark on what was effectively a blank slate of a soul?

Eileen, as if by meticulous design, remained forever south of satisfying in those three areas: seeing, accepting, loving. My first experience with her was a perfect snapshot of the following year, a photograph stretched and distorted over miles both wide and vertical—the range of pleasure and abuse, apologies and fresh starts, predictable relapses, emotional and physical suffering.

One day she brought a brown paper bag to my apartment. I had fixed an Italian meal, and bought a bottle of expensive wine I knew she liked. When she arrived, I leaned in to hug her, but she threw up a hand.

"None of that tonight, sugar. We've got other plans." She held up the bag. There was no levity in her voice or manner. She was simply dark.

I pointed at the bag. "What's that?"

"You'll see."

I waved her in and observed her attire. Casual pants and a tattered sweater. Her hair, too, appeared freshly slept on and she wore only lipstick on her face. I was unable to detect her usual floral scent, instead smelling only dingy hair and a hint of armpit. While I had been feeling confident before her arrival, once more she had caught me off-guard and I found myself floundering. I guided her to the table.

"Candles," she said. "Huh."

"And lasagna. Look, I made it myself."

"Jeepers, Beaver, it's too bad I already ate."

I tried not to let her see how truly deflated I was. I sucked in a slow breath, fought the anger, buried the compulsion to cry, hated myself for wanting to cry.

"Come on," she said. "Let me show you what I brought." There was something new in her voice. Mild excitement perhaps, but if so, it was riding on the back of menace.

I followed her to my bedroom and stood behind her as she reached into her bag.

"We may need some Vaseline," she said as she turned, a length of curved, polished wood in her hand, like a large banana. She shrugged, spoke dully, "Or olive oil, if you want to stick with your Italian theme."

"What's that for?" I suspected I knew, but hoped I was wrong.

"The rectum, Geoffrey. Now hurry up, I have to leave in an hour."

"I am not going to put that in you, Eileen. I'm sorry but I am *not*."

She snapped. "Fuck a nun, Geoffrey! I am so tired of your sissy whining! I don't know how long you think I'm going to put up with this. You're such a little girl! Now just get undressed and get me some goddamn Vaseline or oil."

The saddest part ... Well, prior traumatic events aside, there are still numerous ... The first: I complied with her. Second, the wooden sex tool was not for her, but me. Third, this was not the only time I succumbed to Eileen's demands. I just couldn't let her leave me. Her occasional impulse to hurt me was equal to my need to keep her happy. To keep her.

When she left that night she did not appear in any way satisfied or less angry, as if this was some dirty business she had to get done and now it was done and now she could finally go home. I was in significant pain for several days after, afraid to go see a doctor. How does one explain such injuries? If you're me, you don't. You keep them to yourself and pray for the best.

Pray ...

I wondered what God thought of me, and then, in horror, tried to expunge all thoughts of Him from my head. I shouldn't have been thinking about Him at that moment. What if God has the ability to see everything, but only actually pays attention if you think about Him or pray? Could my actions—my choices—truly determine if I went to heaven or hell? Or was the opportunity for either no longer available to me?

The philosopher Empedocles wrote that he had become a daimon as *punishment*, that he was now this wanderer cursed to move from body to body for thousands of years due to *sin*. His sin, he thought, was cannibalism, having eaten meat from an animal, and since he believed that souls traveled not just between human bodies, but those of animals as well, eating flesh of any sort was cannibalism. His definitions of sin didn't need to match mine for us to feel equally cursed. Even if I didn't count my stepfather, Grant Beauchamp, as a sin, I had taken a young man, Rip, for my own purposes, wiped his mind and left him to die. I ended the life of the mechanic, Tucker, then ran away and killed Jerome Johns. I stole years of life from others, told lies every day of my existence, deliberately obliterated the mind of Tinker so I could feel better about keeping his body for the long term. I ignored my instincts and morals when it came to Eileen, desecrating her body and mine. For as righteous as I thought myself to be, it's pretty damning when you stack it all up like that. If anyone was doomed to hell, it was me.

But if my state was a curse, what was my sin *before* Mr. Beauchamp killed me? Or did the sin even need to occur beforehand? What if time is only visible to us, and God sees all time—past, present, and future? Could one be punished for decisions they would later make? Quincy would have incisive wisdom on the matter. He always did. He would have the answers, know where to look, or he'd ask the right questions to make me see for myself. But Quincy was the last person I wanted to be thinking about.

I constantly struggled with these sorts of thoughts when I was with Eileen. She was like a slow-acting poison I willingly sucked through a straw, little by little, each swallow killing a small part of my soul. She was some dark-tinted mirror in which I only saw the most detestable me.

When she showed up at my apartment a few nights after that particular evening of trauma, she arrived in full Eileen perfection, but with a look of remorse—an expression one might wear when apologizing for forgetting a birthday or anniversary. She stepped in with a pouting lip, her puppy dog eyes fixed on mine.

"Forgive me?"

I wanted to say, "No, I do *not* forgive you! You are not a forgivable person! I never want to see you again! Get out!"

Instead, I shrugged and looked away. In my mind, I had at least triumphed by not saying "yes." But to have said either yes or no would have been stronger than a shrug and silence. I was a small, pitiful thing, and I allowed her to make me smaller and more pitiful each day.

"Well, I know you're probably still mad at me, but I'm going to make it up to you. You know you're my favorite person in the whole wide world!"

I turned away, walking to the sofa. I tried to move normally, to hide the pain that each step sent shooting through my backside, but she saw it at once and rushed to me.

"Oh my dear, Geoffrey!" She placed a gentle hand on my shoulder, stopping me. "You're in agony! I'm so sorry, my sweet!" She turned me around, put her hands over my ears, and attacked my face with kisses. Her eyes seemed to plead with mine for forgiveness. "Come in here, come on." She led me to the bathroom. "I'm going to take care of you."

Eileen squatted in front of the cabinet beneath the sink and found the tub of Vaseline. My muscles all tensed at the sight of it. I stepped back. "Eileen, I don't want—"

"Shush." She stood up and pointed me toward the bedroom. "Unless you have some nitroglycerin ointment, this is the best thing to handle your issues down there. Trust me. I'll never hurt you again."

"It's all right," I continued to argue. "I'll take care of it myself. You don't need to ... ." But I saw her face begin to turn and I stopped resisting. I had to fight my fear and shame, do what she wanted.

Fortunately, as I lay face down on my bed, pants and shorts down around my ankles, Eileen tenderly applied the Vaseline to the enflamed area, quietly humming a children's song. She was like a kind school nurse tending to a scraped knee. It was humiliation on top of degradation, but somehow my relief at not being further violated twisted into blissful appreciation for her. She truly *cared*.

"There you go, my poor baby. Let's get you up now, nice and slow." She helped me slide off the bed, pulled my pants up for me so I wouldn't have to bend or crouch, and then she fastened the buttons and tucked in my shirt. A motherly little smile remained on her face while she looked me over as if she'd just dressed her child for church. Her eyes rose to meet mine. "Now, I told you I would make it up to you. Let's first get that belly full, yes?"

I nodded.

She indeed made it up to me—first with delicious takeout food she'd brought, fed to me as she sat nude at my side. She served me cola on ice and, with a loving wink, wiped it with a washcloth when the glass grew sweaty. She cleaned the table and then guided me to my recliner chair. After placing a soft pillow down, she unfastened my pants, slid them to my feet, and helped me to slowly sit. What followed was an endless, tender ritual throughout which only *I* was to receive pleasure.

Night and day. These contradictions and swings were my world for a little over a year.

"You're like a woman!" she screams.

"I think I've fallen for you," she whispers.

"Shut up! You're a fucking yowling cat! You're not a man!"

"I don't want anybody else but you. I'm going to change. I want to keep you forever."

"I'll never do that to you again."

"I always knew you were queer! I fucking hate you. You're nothing!"

When it was good, I knew it wouldn't last, but I cherished it, certain that the hat would drop at any moment, as it always did.

But I do not wish to leave the impression that there was no good, that there were no *pure* moments between us, because there were many. In the summer, Eileen surprised me one Saturday morning by waking me up with breakfast in bed. Well, she actually woke me in a different manner—one much more pleasurable, but when I later exited the shower, she had breakfast awaiting me on a tray in my bed. She was in one of her great moods, those rare instances during which I could truly relax around her, and she had a surprise for me.

We took the train to Union Square, waited for the station to clear, and then Eileen placed a finger over her lips.

"Shhh." My hand in her hand, we traveled down halls and through doors, ending up in a seemingly defunct subway tunnel.

"Eileen, do you know where—?"

"Shhh." was all she'd say.

Eventually, we arrived in a grandiose station with Romanesque architecture unlike any other subway station I'd seen. A skylight glowed overhead through ornate glasswork, and immaculate green and white tile covered every inch of wall or archway. We were the only people present; the only sounds were the muffled whirs and toots of distant trains, and the vague rumble of vehicles passing overhead.

"What is this place?" I whispered.

"City Hall Station," she said. "And you don't have to whisper. Been closed for more than a decade. I hoped you'd never been. What do you think?"

"It's amazing!" I spun slowly around. "Are we *allowed* to be in here?"

"Moot. Fuck 'em. We're here, aren't we? Maybe we got lost." She shrugged and looked at my face, which was surely beaming. "I'm so happy!" she proclaimed and it echoed through the place. I looked in her eyes and we kissed for a time, my hand on the back of her head. She reached between my legs and began to rub up and down, pulled her mouth off mine, and asked, "You wanna fuck?" And oddly enough, I did. And we did, right there on the stairs.

The day continued: lunch in Greenwich, afternoon at the park, dinner in Little Italy, and it all ended free of incident (other than our waiter potentially hearing Eileen refer to him as a "wop").

It was one for the books.

The next day went bad, but I was mostly fine with it. That Saturday would keep me going through at least a few days of hell.

Over time, I had learned Eileen's triggers and avoided them at all cost. If she found something mildly interesting or humorous, I had to enjoy it more, find it fascinating, hilarious. If she offered hints as to what she wanted or needed at any given moment, I only had one job: *decipher those clues ... and fast*. And don't ask questions—just keep throwing those darts until one happens to hit the bull's-eye.

In the fall of 1960, having completed my degree programs in record time, I began work on my Master's thesis: "A New Look at the Pre-Socratics." I had huge plans for this paper: combining— as opposed to contrasting—the outlooks of ancient philosophers with those of present-day thinkers. I knew it would occupy much more of my time than my previous studies, and I planned to work on it with Stan and at the library (as often as I could get away with), but I hadn't accurately predicted the intensity of Eileen's reaction to my divided focus.

* * *

"Booooring!"

Eileen was not thrilled with my preoccupation. My thesis final draft was seventy-five percent complete, and I had to stop discussing it in any way around her. I had to give up trying to share any of my work or theories with Eileen, receiving only exaggerated yawns and moans.

"You're killing me with this crap!" she'd say as she plucked the last leaves of basil from the plant I'd spent months cultivating.

"Words, words, words!" screamed in my ear.

"Why would anybody care about this shit?" Unnumbered papers fly into the air.

"I'm out of here. I don't fuck nerds or squares." She tips her red wine glass over my sofa's taupe upholstery.

I don't know why I kept trying as long as I had. I suppose I had thought each time that the subject would grab her, show her there *were* parts of my studies that she could appreciate. As with most things Eileen, I had been slow to grasp her absolute disinterest. But at some point I accepted her utter disdain for academics and my voice (when it spoke anything other than words about her, or words she insisted I say while we made love), and I stopped trying. It didn't feel good, but there was no way I would be able to complete my thesis around Eileen. I had to back off for a while and hope for the best when I was ready to return my full attention to her. My sudden silence exposed a previously unseen side to her.

"Did you see my pedicure? My feet are perfect, you know."

"Did you know that beauty is when things are balanced? It's called symmetrics. I have perfect symmetrics. Look."

"You know I'm way out of your league, right? I mean, look at me. Only joking. You're cute."

"I'm thinking of changing my hair. Audrey Hepburn got a short cut. Would you like that better?"

Silence didn't work in these scenarios. An answer was required. I always felt trapped and confounded by the questions that could go either way. "Yes, your feet are very clearly perfect." That's an easy one. But choices were dangerous, and in my experience, my choices were never the right ones. "I think the short cut would look wonderful."

"So you don't like my hair? You've *never* liked my hair?"

The public berating got to me the most. On more than one occasion she screamed obscenities at me in the middle of a crowd and slapped me or kicked me in the shin.

Realizing that even our weekend time together was impairing my work and wrecking my brain, I grew still more distant. I made myself less available. I would tell Eileen I couldn't see her on some specific night, but she would frequently show up anyway. No longer able to get any research done with her around, I spent more time at Stan's, as I had him proofreading and reviewing my research notes. Often, she would tell me on the telephone that she had shown up at my apartment, how she had *really* needed to be with me. I'd always say I had been at Stan's.

Fortunately for me (and Stan), despite knowing I could often be found there, Eileen never came looking for me at Stan's. And her apartment was not only in the same building as his, but on the same floor. Stan was 4G, and she was 4A. Occasionally, when leaving Stan's I would walk to her door, contemplate knocking. But generally by that time I was spent, and just wanted to sleep. Sleep wouldn't be in the cards if I knocked on that door.

Don't get me wrong, I was still terrified that she would leave me. I remained very much in her trap, hoping to be with her for the foreseeable future. But I was truly exhausted and simply didn't have the energy to deal with her. My plan was to get my thesis behind me and then redirect my focus back on her. I would surely pay for a week or two, but then things would return to their normal ups and downs.

During the week my thesis was due, I called Eileen and informed her I wouldn't be able to see her at all, but would make it up by taking her out to a great dinner that weekend. She sounded wholly understanding, wished me luck, and we agreed on a time for Saturday night. It was utter naiveté for me to take her amicable response at face value.

My thesis turned in for review and my presentation to the committee booked, I scheduled my date with Eileen. She sounded elated over the phone. I dressed up in my best suit, bought flowers from a street vendor, and knocked on her door. No answer. I knocked again. Nothing, but I thought I heard sounds through the door. I turned the knob to see if it was unlocked, and it rotated a full quarter turn, the door swinging open before me.

The sounds gained definition. Grunts and slapping. My breath stopped. Blood rushed from my head. I took two steps in and peered around the corner toward her bedroom. The lights were on; throw pillows littered the floor. Eileen's red silk bedspread lay crumpled on the hardwood below the feet of the colored man laying in her bed. Eileen was on top of him, bouncing up and down, her rear end facing me, her pale skin a stark contrast to the colored man's dark legs and member.

The flowers dropped to the ground with a soft rustle, but Eileen heard and spun her head around. There was no surprise on her face, only that clever little smile, and she continued riding up and down on the man.

"Oh, hey you! Were we supposed to go out *tonight?*"

I turned and walked out of the apartment.

She called after me, "Wait, I'm almost done!"

My ears felt the pressure of swimming in a deep pool, garbled cries in my head, a looping visual of a dark brown penis dis- and re-appearing, the satisfaction in her eyes. She had sentenced me to the ultimate punishment for my selfish, inattentive behavior.

I walked.

Two hours later I was on the Third Avenue Bridge, looking out over the Harlem River and found myself once more wondering if it was possible for me to die, and if I could, where would I go? If only I was able to wipe my own memories.

* * *

Eileen called and showed up repeatedly the following week, but I simply hung up without a word or ignored her pleading at my door. One night, she showed up past 1:00AM and would not leave the hall outside my apartment. She knocked three times every minute and slowly sang "Geoffrey ... ." After twenty minutes of it, I got dressed and descended the fire escape, fleeing to Stan's. I let myself in with the spare key and crashed on his couch without waking him.

In the morning, I awoke to a tapping on my shoulder.

"Crazy lady?" he said with a pitying smirk.

I nodded. "One in the morning."

"I don't know, buddy. I think you need to see her. Talk it over. Let her get out whatever's built up in her system. Otherwise, who knows how far off the deep end she can go?"

"You might be right."

"Hey, I'm just glad she hasn't come banging on my door, but that doesn't mean she never will."

I considered what I could do. Talking on the phone seemed the safest, but I didn't even want to do that. Any contact would just give her an opportunity to punish *me* for "making her" have relations with that man. It would end up my fault somehow, and even if I ended it, the only way for it to be clean would be for me to admit some sort of wrongdoing. I simply couldn't do that to myself. I had to leave in a strong position, or I could never respect myself again.

A thought occurred to me. I asked Stan, "Have you seen her with any other men?"

"Nope ... not really. Hell, I only ever saw the two of you together once through my window here. Shows you how much I get out. Tell you what though ... Kinda sorry to say it, but I'm just glad you found out how loony this broad is. I would've been hitting on her to the end of time, and this coulda been me."

I smiled. "Appreciate the support, Stan."

He clapped my back. I realized then—or I should say, I appreciated once more—that I had Stan. He, more than anyone before or after, *saw* me and *appreciated* me. We were great friends. I liked to think we had some sort of platonic, camaraderic *love*. Having a woman was fulfilling for certain, but I realized that in the future, as long as I had Stan, I didn't need to seek out in mates all of those things that I needed for happiness. I could never actually *tell* him that, for as close as we were, we would never discuss such things, but I was okay with that. Remaining unspoken didn't render it any less real.

The following week, while still awaiting the thesis committee's acceptance of my work, I was going over my oral defense, to be presented in just a few days. My telephone rang around 6:30 in the evening. I picked up.

"Geoffrey?" Eileen sounded woozy. "Is that you?"

I pulled the receiver an inch from my ear. I needed to hang up fast, but I hesitated.

She went on, "Took these pills ... I'm dying ... I just wanted to tell you good-bye and that I'm sorry ... ."

I pressed the phone back to my ear. "Eileen? You took pills? What did you take?"

"I don't know ... ." She snickered a little—her slow, drunk voice. "Little of this, little of that ... A *lot* of that, ashwly ... mmmm ... I love you so much ... I realized I just have to let you go, let you be free. I'm such a bad person. You've been nothing but good to me and I just hold you back. The whole world will be better off if I was dead, you especially ... I know this now ... don't tr't'stp me, gffwy ... mmmm ... ."

Her phone fell and clacked around before disconnecting. I dialed the operator and asked to be transferred to the police . "…It's an emergency!"

Eileen was driven by ambulance to Lincoln Hospital in South Bronx. I arrived there shortly after her, and located her by the shrill sound of profanity and racial epithets ("It's the fucking truth, you tramp … This many niggers in one place can lead to nothing good!")

I walked into the room, Eileen flanked by two nurses, one colored, one white. Eileen appeared in perfect health, if a bit bedraggled. She spotted me at once.

"Oh thank the luck, Geoffrey, you came! You have to get me out of here! I could be raped at any second! This is a colored hospital!"

I muttered, "I'm sure you'll be fine, Eileen," and looked at the nurses. "Can I speak with one of you, please?"

The white nurse nodded to her colleague, offering her an escape from Eileen. She followed me out the door and around the corner. I turned to her and looked at her name badge. Dubois.

"Your wife, sir?" Nurse Dubois asked.

"No. Girlfriend. But … but not anymore. She's, well, as you saw. She called me, after the pills. I was the one that called the police."

"Well, sir, then you would probably be interested to know the tests found no signs of drug overdose. All of her vital signs were completely normal." She saw me clench my jaw and shake my head. She leaned closer. "We get this sometimes, you know. Someone cuts their wrists, but only a *little bit*, you know. We say 'suicide attempt' in docs, but everyone here knows what that means. Person wants to kill themselves for real, they're usually successful. Get me?"

"Did you tell her all that? I mean, about the tests?"

"Yes, the doctor told her he found nothing dangerous in her system. She told him to check again, and to not have any 'ignorant niggers' involved this time."

"I see. I'm awfully sorry about her ... her words ... and *her*, too, I suppose. So what now?"

"We let her go when the doctor says she can go. You have no obligation to stay here or take her home. But I tell you what, sir ... You're the one she called. That means if you leave her here after *this* ... it sure ain't gonna be the end of it. Expect something worse next time."

"No, I won't leave her here. Thank you ... and sorry again."

"Oh that nonsense doesn't bother me, sir. The more crazy white ladies I meet, the better I feel about being a colored one." She winked and walked off down the hall.

"Geoffrey? Are you out there? Geoffrey!"

I helped her to fill out paperwork, paid an exorbitant bill, and Eileen was released. I got us a taxi and walked her up to her apartment.

"I'm probably in no condition to—" she began, her makeup smeared eyes attempting a seductive glance.

Utterly through with her, I interrupted, "Take care of yourself, Eileen," and walked back down the hall. I expected her to scream after me, but instead she spoke softly.

"Is this really what you want?"

I turned. "Yes. I think it's best for both of us."

Her eyes drifted down to the floor, her fingers tickling the sides of her dress. "Would it change your mind if I told you I was pregnant?"

It couldn't be true. I didn't believe it. Her desperation would lead her to say whatever she thought might manipulate me into staying with her. But I didn't want to set her off again. I needed it to end clean.

"Let's go to lunch tomorrow," I said. "We'll talk things over, okay?"

A small glimmer in her eye, a barely concealed glint of triumph. "That sounds good."

"Burger joint up the street? Noon?"

She smiled wide and her eyes went glassy. She took a deep breath. "I think that's the most *perfect* choice you could ever make. I love you, Geoffrey. Just remember that I'm the only one that truly sees you."

She'd never spoken the word "love" with any sincerity before, but it wasn't working. There was nothing she could say to erase what I'd seen in her bedroom that day. In fact, I was grateful to her for providing me that release. The permission to go. Who knows how long I would have put up with her abuse if I hadn't walked in on that scene? The only tricky part left was to keep alive some small amount of hope. To make a definitive statement that it was over forever would surely light an inextinguishable fuse. The detonation would surely be unprecedented. But to offer her *too much* hope would be wrong and eventually lead back down the exact path she had just traveled. I needed to make it clear we were separating and not seeing each other for *at least* a couple weeks. At *some point* after that, we could "see how both of us felt."

I just prayed she wouldn't see through it.

I wanted to walk straight down the hall to Stan's and tell him the whole sordid tale, but I couldn't have Eileen knowing I was still in the building. I predicted she would watch the street from her window, see me appear on the sidewalk, cross to the subway, disappear below. I thought of crafty ways I could circle round the building, sneak to his apartment, but the risk of her catching me was too great. And what would she think, seeing me creep toward Stan's door? No, I decided to go all the way home and call him, instead. It was only 10:45 and he usually stayed up until 11:00.

"So what are you going to tell her?" Stan asked.

"I'm going to make like I just need a break, you know. For *both* of us."

"Riiiight. That's smart. You don't want her to go bonkers on you again."

"Exactly what I was thinking."

"Well, bring me a burger when you're done with her. On that biscuit bun. Loaded with mustard."

"I'll see what I can do."

* * *

Eileen never showed up to the burger joint. She didn't answer to knocking on her door. She never answered her phone. On Monday, the bank where she worked said she hadn't come in and did not call. Stan hadn't seen her around the building since the prior week, but he hadn't been looking before I told him she was missing.

"I'll keep an eye out, buddy. You think you should call the police?"

"I don't know."

I didn't. If it was another game, I'd be playing right into it. And with Tinker's history, the last thing I ever wanted was to be talking to the police. He had committed numerous crimes in Kansas, Missouri, and Oklahoma, served time for many. And those were the only states I had checked. If they did some digging on me and found what I had, the police would be idiots to believe anything I told them. No, I would not be calling the police. I would look for her myself, as was surely her plan.

8. Tides

It is a fascinating human characteristic the ability to instantly change one's priorities, or rather, to instantly adapt as they are altered by circumstance. I think it's both an indication of our natural flexibility and our true insignificance—simply kelp swaying as the tide demands. One day, you strive toward a promotion, grow bitter as you're once more overlooked, wanting nothing more than this wrong to be righted. The next day your house is flooded, robbed, destroyed by a hurricane, or burned down. A loved one gets bad news from their doctor. Your child is drafted into the Army to be sent away to war.

Is life's purpose to fight the tides as much as possible, or to sway with them, play by other's rules, go with the flow? Or is the very idea of some predefined intent a fallacy, an ancient straw-grasping, borne of our desperation to understand that which is not understandable? If you're kelp, you can't fight the tides. If there is such a thing as destiny, why bother ever doing anything? We sway where we are forced to sway; it doesn't matter what we consider a priority.

A week earlier, I had considered my Master of Arts thesis the most important thing in my world. My girlfriend of fourteen months was not only a low priority, but I considered her a hindrance to happiness—a sick, life-sucking drain on my very soul. Seven days later, she still hadn't returned to her apartment. Now, she was the one love of my life, witty and impossibly beautiful, if a bit sensitive. That was the *real* problem, right? She was delicate, and I didn't handle her with the proper care. How could I have treated her that way, this goddess that had opted to bless a lowly man like me with her companionship? She could have had anybody in the world, but she chose me. I had to find her, and I would be a different person—a good person, a great lover—if I could just find her and set things right. And if I did all that, she would have no reason to do the sorts of things she used to do to hurt me. Right?

I'm not so sure I had myself convinced of the latter, but circumstance had certainly blurred a bit of my animosity toward her, and the good times had suddenly shone brighter than before in my memory.

Stan had convinced the building manager to unlock her door for me and I saw that her place appeared as it always did. Not too messy, but not exactly tidy. The animal print rugs lay in their usual places. Her sink was empty of dishes and dry, as it always was. Her pile of stones remained atop her fake mantle, a columnal plaster structure set against the living room wall with artificial logs that lit up orange when activated. The rocks had seemed out of place among the rest of her décor and I'd asked her about them early on.

"Those are the stones I would have thrown at Jesus," she'd said with no apparent emotion.

It was before I knew her feelings on religion. I asked, "As in, like the others, before they knew he was God?" I ran my fingers over a hunk of granite at the top and thought the pile a brilliant, humble piece to have in one's home. A constant reminder of imperfection, a warning against judgment of others.

"No, not really," she'd replied and peered into her refrigerator.

The building manager went to the door. "I have to go unclog a shower drain. Mind locking up when you leave?"

Stan and I agreed and I walked into the bedroom.

All of her clothes were there. Her suitcase, hat boxes, and jewelry I knew she treasured, all undisturbed. Fear and guilt washed over me. How could I think it was all a ploy? What kind of human being was I to not at least call the police—get *someone* investigating? I was selfish, and if she was indeed kidnapped, as all indicators suggested, then whatever happened to her after she didn't show up for our lunch date—the one in which I would break up with her— would be *my* responsibility.

As we perused her apartment, Stan didn't help any: "This doesn't look good, Geoff. You really should'a called the cops."

After seeing all of her things in her apartment, I finally did alert the authorities.

An officer came, had a look around, and took my statement. He didn't appear suspicious of me at first, but when I couldn't provide information about Eileen's family or other friends, his questions turned to me. I told the truth, that I was originally from California, omitting any mention of the Midwest states where Tinker had roamed.

He asked if anything out of the ordinary had occurred in the weeks prior to her disappearance. He asked if Eileen and I were having any issues. I did my best to tell all non-incriminating truths:

no, we didn't really argue. Yes, she had sort of attempted suicide. No, it had nothing to do with me. Yes, we had been seeing less of each other. No, I had never struck her.

And then the dreaded question: "Either of you ever carry on with someone else?"

"I most certainly did not. I cannot speak to what I don't know about Eileen."

He raised an eyebrow. "What's that mean, 'you cannot speak to'?"

"Meaning, I don't know."

He held his gaze, unconvinced, before jotting more notes.

The officer took down all of my information: address, telephone number, employer. He wanted all the names of my friends and family. I told him I only had Stan and my coworkers, and claimed I was an orphan. I began to think again that calling the police was a mistake. They would shine a tight beam on me and not seek other leads. I needed to find her myself or figure out what happened, and fast.

I prayed to God to bring her back to me. I apologized for my sins, and for being what I was, if it was as a result of anything I had done. I prayed to every God I'd ever heard of, apologizing to each for any offense I may have caused in addressing other deities, or for my faith ever wavering. I made more promises. I sang Eileen's praises while laying myself at their mercy.

I was in crisis, and nothing else seemed to matter anymore.

* * *

Eileen walked through Morningside Park on her way to work every day. I had called her work number and a receptionist told me she hadn't shown up to work in over a week. Why would she still come through the park? It made little sense, but I had nowhere else to look. My alarming lack of acquaintance with her life—beyond our shared meals and frequent lovemaking—had dropped on my head like a piano. How had it never seemed strange to me? Then again, everything seemed strange in our relationship, why would that part stand out? I was never comfortable, always caught off-guard, forever clinging to whatever I could grasp.

All morning, I sat on a bench in the park along the path I knew Eileen used to walk. I tried to appear nonchalant with my newspaper as my eyes flashed to each passing face.

I was startled when a voice spoke behind me.

"Oh-so-many faces." It sounded deep and inhuman, like the voice a father would use for the monster in a bedtime fairytale.

I cringed and turned. "I beg your pardon?"

He stood with his hands in his brown slacks, his shoulders slumped and fedora'd head held low. Even hunching as he did, like a giant, starved vulture, he was by far the tallest man I'd ever seen. His smiling face was long and bony, an exaggeration of features one would only find in caricature. Bulbous chin, massive jaw, overly pronounced brow, sallow skin. My expression surely betrayed my shock, and his sedate grin revealed he was accustomed to such reactions to his appearance. I fought the compulsion to apologize.

"So many faces, I says." There was an accent—perhaps Eastern European—partially obscured by the deep bass. "To look at each one ... ach ... exhausting."

I shrugged and shook my head with nothing to say in reply. He stepped from the grass to the paved path in front of me; his stilt-like legs looked more exhausting to haul around than simply watching passers-by. His pant cuffs hung more than a few inches above his brown socks. Beneath his matching jacket he wore a yellow oxford with a thin paisley tie.

"I am Gregor." He held out his hand, long and knuckley, with perfect yet too-long nails. "I am foreign."

I shook it. His skin felt powdery.

I shifted and he sat down beside me, inquiring as to whether I was searching for anyone in particular. I pulled the photo of Eileen from my coat pocket and he squinted to make it out. After a moment of low humming, he licked his teeth and snapped a conclusive nod.

"I saw this young lady yesterday enter the subway with colored man. One Hundred Third Street."

Shocked, I stammered, "You're certain it was her?"

He tilted his elongated neck to the side, adjusted his hat. "If you know this woman yourself, then you know why I remember her."

It was true. Eileen stood out to everyone, man or woman. When we were together, all eyes would study her, entranced, and then shift to me. Women always appeared intrigued, observing something remarkable in me that, absent Eileen, they would have never seen. Men's reactions were different, their faces betraying their envy: "What the hell does that poor shlub have to deserve *her*?" Or they would appear to dismiss me as only a friend, often approaching her as if I wasn't there. "Well hello there, beautiful ...

." Depending on her mood, Eileen might toy with the men, shaming me with her flirtation, or pull me closer and say to them "You don't got a chance, buster."

The strange man handed the photograph back to me, still nodding.

"Seen her before then. I get my paper from Benny's newsstand on Park. Benny's an A-rab, but good man, no doubts. I see this one," he poked the photograph with a fingernail, "always looking at the girl magazine. Just the cover, but every one of them. There when I get there, there when I leave."

Eileen was obsessed with models and magazines. I'd seen her do this myself, studying the makeup of the cover models, their expressions, clothes.

"Which newsstand was this?" I asked.

"Benny's. Just down Park," He pointed past me. "He's an A-rab, but don't worry. Good man. Maybe you ask him if he saw her, too? Maybe with colored man, too." He made a *but I'm sure they are just acquaintances* gesture, so as not to suggest some impropriety on her part.

I shook my head and stood up to face him. "Now tell me again, you saw her where? When? Just the last time. The subway?"

"I repeat once and say again, my friend. One Hundred Third Street. Yesterday."

I stammered, "Was ... Was she all right? Or ... Or, how can you be so sure it was her? Did she appear frightened?"

Gregor rose with unexpected zip, pinched the brim of his hat. "She appeared ... *insouciant.* Best of luck."

I called after him but did not follow. "What does *that* mean? Was it morning? Afternoon? Was the man—" But he either did not hear or chose to ignore me. I didn't call out again or try to chase him down. I should have, but I was afraid. Afraid he spoke the truth; afraid it was a lie or a mistake, afraid of *him*. I should have at least asked his last name, address, given them to the police. They would certainly never believe my description of him, and the story, that of a strange man in the park that happened to have seen Eileen, would work against me. They would think I'd made it up to demonstrate my innocence. *See, I shouldn't be a suspect ... There may not even be a crime.*

I crumpled back down onto the bench with fatigue, despair, fear. Thoughts raced through my mind. Guilty presumptions ... She's simply moved in with that man I saw her with. Fears about what might have happened to her last week if this foreign man was mistaken about yesterday. I just hoped, whatever happened, that she wasn't scared. The idea of her frightened—in some terrible situation—made me feel ill. She seemed like a strong person on the outside, but I knew how truly fragile she was inside.

I watched a series of faces pass for a bit before I decided to go talk to this newsstand guy the foreigner had mentioned. I walked to Park and asked around until I found someone who knew where "Benny's" was. Only a few more blocks south.

Benny's newsstand was not very well stocked, and Benny was asleep when I got there, a flat cap pulled down over his eyes. Customers simply tossed change into a can on the counter when buying the paper or a magazine. They could have all been pennies, for all he knew.

I leaned into the window. "Sir, may I ask you a question?"

He stirred a little, popped one eye open, then promptly returned to his dreams. I repeated myself, louder and he shimmied himself out like a wet duck.

"Dofuhyuh?!" he shouted, but his accent was distinctly Brooklyn, not remotely Arab. He was tan, and had a bushy black moustache.

I held out the photo of Eileen. "Have you seen this lady?" He pursed his lips as he considered it. "Maybe in the last week? Name's Eileen."

"Yeah, I seen'er. Most every day."

"You seen her today?" I pressed. "Today or yesterday?"

He rocked his head side to side and turned his eyes up to recall.

"If not today then yesterday f'sure. Looks at the girls, sometimes actually buys one, but I don't mind much, y'know? Good f'business, that one. Sticky-eyed fellas end up buyin' whatever it was they picked up as an excuse to hang 'round a bit longer. Gotta love the ol' upside-down newspaper readin', y'know?" He chuckled and adjusted his hat.

"Listen, if you see her again, can you give her a message for me?" He shrugged acceptance. "Please tell her that Geoffrey needs to speak with her *urgently*." I thought about what she might want to hear—what could pique her interest. "And tell her I've figured it all out. That there's so much we have to discuss."

"So Geoffrey's gotta talk to her and *you*'ve got stuff figured out. Who are you?"

"I'm Geoffrey."

He play-slapped his forehead. "Oh, *you're* Geoffrey! Okay, that makes more sense. 'Geoffrey's got it all figured out, urgently need to talk.'"

"Good enough. Thank you, sir. I appreciate it."

He tipped his hat, crossed his arms, and reclined back into his chair, eyes closed.

I headed back uptown for the subway station the foreign man had mentioned. I sat for hours on the steps of the 103rd Street stairway, flicking through faces until they all looked the same. When the autumn sun began to set, I took the train up to South Bronx then back down to East Harlem.

"Mr. Cuion," the Detective said as he stepped up the curb. I flinched. I'd been walking in a daze. Three uniformed officers stood at the ready behind him. The police had apparently been waiting in a van outside my building. He touched my elbow. "Or should I call you *Tinker?*"

Well, it's all over now, I thought.

* * *

The mustachioed Detective Morton dropped a cardboard box onto the table in front of me, its contents rattling and clanking.

"Guess where all this came from, *Tinker.*"

"That's not my name. I don't know why you people keep calling me that."

"Uh-huh."

"And I have no idea what you have there."

His hand disappeared into the box, emerging a second later with a pair of handcuffs dangling from his index finger.

"You're not in law enforcement, now, are you, Mr. Cuion?"

"No. And those are not mine. They're Eileen's."

"They were in your bed table. Along with," he reached in with his other hand, "this."

He extracted Eileen's leather crop whip.

With a disgusted smirk, Detective Morton said, "You ride horses when you're not policing?"

I shook my head and looked away. "I'm sure everything you have in there is Eileen's. She had ... *different* sorts of tastes."

Detective Morton turned to the other officer in the interrogation room, a lanky bird-faced man whose name I never caught. They shared a knowing look before Morton sat down across the table from me, gloating and smug.

"You know what's interesting about talking to murderers?" He waited for me to answer as if the question were not rhetorical. I sat silent, expressionless. "You start to catch little things ... like a *tell* in cards. You play cards?" I waited. He eventually continued. "See, when we talk to a *real* concerned relative that ain't done nothing wrong, they want to believe their loved one is gonna make it home all right. They don't wanna think of the horrible things that might'a happened. They just got lost, or stuck somewhere, and ... here's the key: they say stuff like, 'She *has* a friend in Jersey, or he *works* at the docks.' I glanced at the bird-faced officer and received a haughty eyebrow pop. Geniuses. They just had it all figured out. "But see a *killer*, they know there ain't no way their vic's showing up alive. They say, 'She *had* a bad habit of gettin' lost. She *was* always hangin' round the wrong sort.' Get it?"

"Brilliant, Detective," I said. "But this time, whatever past-tense verb you heard me use has no bearing on my guilt or innocence as—"

"Funny you said 'my guilt' first."

"…I have committed no crimes. I have been searching for her for the past week. You can ask my friend, Stanley Bush. He can also attest to Eileen's … Her *private* side."

"Why? He poking her too?"

"What? No! He knows … I told him all about … ." I hesitated. "I told him some of the things she wanted us to do."

"Oh, I see. So you want us to confirm your story by going to your friend and asking him if *you* ever *told* him about this kind'a sex stuff." He pulled out the banana-shaped length of wood. "You put *this* in her?"

I sighed and turned away. I would not be answering any more questions about our sexual activities. Besides the utter humiliation of it, if they considered perversion in general to be incriminating, the truth of who did what to whom would surely prove to be motive enough for them.

"Hey!" Detective Morton slapped me on the side of the head, knocking my glasses off and sending a lightning bolt of pain through my ear, which immediately began ringing. "I asked you a fucking question, scumbag!"

I held my ear for a moment and fought the screaming urge to wipe his mind. I looked at him through a blurry glaze of tears. "Am I under arrest?"

He barked, "Yes, you're under arrest! What the hell do you think you're doing here? We know all about Kansas and Missouri,

Tinker. You think we're gonna let you walk outta here and ride outta town? Go hide somewhere else?"

"I haven't been read my rights."

The other officer finally spoke up. He was disconcertingly soft spoken. "You ain't got no rights, freak. You're a convict."

"The Constitution of the United States would take—"

Another slap from Morton, this time square on my cheek, the bones in his palm stinging my cheekbone. I sprung from the chair, balled my fists, and glowered. My face burned. Morton looked thrilled. He had his fists in front of him as he rocked back and forth like a boxer.

"You gonna hit me, Tinker? You wanna try and strangle me like I'm your buddy Sergeant Vale? Gimme a chair hat like Deputy Ferguson? They all say you're a real tough guy—a junkyard dog! Lemme see some of that! Don't be shy!"

I realized what he was trying to do. Provoke me into assaulting an officer. It suggested they didn't have enough evidence to hold me. I sat back down.

"A sissy?" Morton spat. "Shit, maybe you ain't Tinker after all. Every single cop you've crossed said to watch out for you. Actually made me a little nervous. No reason for that though, I guess. You're just a little sissy girl, ain'tcha?"

Calling names? I snorted. If that was all he had left, I'd be fine. He cocked back and punched me full strength in the eye. I fell back in the chair, hit my head on the brick wall behind me. "Piece of trash!" he snarled, then kicked the chair into me. More sharp pains jolted through my back. I curled up into a ball in the corner awaiting more punishment, but it didn't come. Instead, I heard the two of them quietly conferring.

"I'll take it. Just be quick," the quiet one said.

"Ack ... don't feel right. You got walloped by that nigger last week. Should be me this time. Just pop me good in the lip. It'll swell right up."

"Wasn't even a big deal, that one—"

A loud rapping on the door. I snuck a peek and caught the same unsure expression on both of their faces.

Morton snapped, "Yeah?"

A muffled younger man's voice returned, "Dickey says a lawyer's on the way back here."

Their uncertainty morphed to fear. They both looked at me.

Morton strode around the table to me. "You call a lawyer, Cuion?" I didn't reply. He pulled me up by the arm. "Huh? When'd you call a lawyer?" I hadn't. I didn't even know any lawyers. The other cop righted the chair and I was plopped back down.

A more official knock sounded through the door.

The same voice: "Detectives, Mr. Queen's attorney is here to speak with him. Shall I have him wait in—" Another muffled voice, but deep—its warbled bass rendering any words indistinguishable. Then the young officer again, "Well ... I don't ... ."

Detective Morton cracked open the door and peered out.

"Sorry, Detective," the young uniformed officer said. "Mr. ... Nemet, is it? Says he has to see his client right now to be—"

"Yes, that is correct," the deep voice boomed and the door swung open the rest of the way. I put my glasses back on and couldn't believe what I was seeing. "Thank you for ensuring my client's safety this evening, detectives. You may be stepping out now while I confer with Mr. Cuion. Oh my. What's happened to you, sir?" The towering, vulturesque man from the park gave me a wink as he set his briefcase on the table. The detectives gaped at the bizarre figure before them, both at a loss for words.

Morton babbled, "He ... ah ... ." and grabbed his own lip, apparently forgetting for an instant that his partner had yet to punch him.

"Well, I'll be conferring with my client about this. You may be going. We'll let you know when we're ready for you."

Flustered, the officers merely gawked at the tall man in the brown suit, unable to express their objections as his expansive arms herded them out the door. The latch clicked and we were alone. He peered over his shoulder at me with a wicked smile and, for a second, I was petrified. His little eyes were like black dimes, bordered by only slightly wider eyelids. The whites only showed when he glanced right or left.

"Gregor," he said, answering the question in my head. He slid a chair back and bent his stilts until seated across from me. "Gregor Német, Attorney at Law. And you are Geoffrey Cuion, I'm led to believe."

Led to believe?

"We met in the park," I said. "How are you here ... How did you know I was arrested? Why are you—"

"Is very strange, I know. I am foreign so used to being misunderstood, but many confusing situations gain perfect clarity when observed with hindsight."

"I don't think I understand at all."

"Of course not." He giggled and wheezed a little. "You are in the middle of the situation and therefore yet have to obtain hindsight. And, in your case, foresight does appear not to be well-honed. You're in the middle."

It might have been the accent or jumbled verbs blurring my comprehension, though he seemed fairly articulate with English. Without being cruel, I thought his real problem with communication was his appearance. I couldn't imagine anyone speaking to this man without being thoroughly preoccupied by that face and head. Some sort of birth deformity, I imagined.

I directed my eyes to the table and replied, "I really have no idea what you're talking about. I mean, I get what you're saying conceptually—I'm a philosophy student—but the situation? The situation is I've been arrested for something I didn't do, but the police have every reason to believe I'm guilty. They won't even bother to look for my girlfriend. Did you tell them you saw her?"

His fingers brushed my question away like a moth; his nose crinkled as from a sour odor. "Pointless. Now, down to business." He opened his briefcase and removed a legal pad and pen. "I am not a criminal attorney, just so you are aware."

"You're not—"

"No. Alas, I work in probate, with the true maggots of society."

"So why—"

"You appeared to require assistance." He peered into the box of Eileen's sundries. "What's all this about?"

I had no interest in sharing those details with him. I didn't even know how he knew I was at the police station, not to mention the fact that he was an utterly unsettling individual. But he had interrupted the officers' plan to set me up, throwing them on the defensive, and that fact did not escape me.

"Listen," I said. "Are you here to represent me? You said you don't do criminal law, but here you are. Please just explain what you're looking to accomplish."

He affected exaggerated disappointment, spoke in a sing-song, "I thought it obvious. I am here to *help* you. Did you wish to spend night, and foreseeable future, incarcerated?"

"Absolutely not."

"But it does appear that is the detectives' plan."

"Yes, it would appear to be. But *you* ... How did you know ... there was just the park—"

"I happened to be passing when you were arrested. I put it together. Not difficult to imagine what they suspected, and I saw truth in your face, the despair, in the park."

He was clearly lying. The odds of him being near my apartment—miles from the park—a ridiculous prospect.

"You followed me. What are you looking for? Are you a friend of Eileen?"

He reclined into the chair, crossed his leg over his knee. "Haha ... *Eileen.*"

"So you do know her."

His smile and gaze held. "The police never will see past you, you know. They don't need to find a body. Unless Ms. Scoville turns up, of course."

"Yes."

"And yet, notwithstanding the eventuality of prison, you have elected to remain here. I am curious. Why?"

Interesting choice of words, I thought, and then I got it. A feeling. Something I'd never felt before. It grabbed me by the chest, sent electric chills all through my body. My face must have shown it because Gregor smiled wide.

"*There* it is," he said and slapped the table. His voice had changed subtly—a bit more squeak among the bass. His accent remained, but the "I is foreign, English be hard" façade disappeared. He was giddy. "I was wondering if you would ever see it. So tell me, what is your real name?"

With no hesitation, breathless, it passed my lips for only the second time in my life, "Samuel."

"Wonderful! The great prophet and judge! Do you know who you are here to save?"

"I beg your—"

"Beg nothing. I joke. Now listen close. You have that nasty little Geoffrey Cuion in there with you?"

"I ... No." My head hung. "It's just me."

He brought his index finger to his lips. "Mmm ... You're one of *those,* eh? I would have never guessed. It matters not, I suppose. Just leave him. Let *them* deal with the flesh sack."

"Just leave? But, the body ... Not just the body ... my *life* ...
"

"This is what I don't understand. Why still here at all with this nonsense? Are you attached to the suit? You *are* ... You must be young. How old are you?"

I had to think a moment. "Twenty-seven, I guess. If you mean—"

"Ah, just a baby! Adorable. I now see your problem. Juveniles always bumble about for decades like they're still one of *them*. You must let that go."

I couldn't believe I was sitting there across from another of my kind. How long had I feared I was alone? And how many others were out there? He said "juveniles," suggesting not only that there were many entities like us, but of all ages, and I was apparently a young one.

For some reason I spoke in a hushed tone, "Do you mind ... Would you mind me asking how old *you* are?"

His chest inflated with pride: he'd be delighted to answer. "I'll be a thousand in a few years. The big four digits."

One thousand! That meant the Middle Ages!

"I have so many questions. I don't know where to begin."

"I'm the first you've met? Fascinating. This should tell you the mindset of your typical demon. Timid and selfish. I assure you that others have seen you."

Demon.

A knock on the door and the head of the young officer poked in. "The detectives wish to resume questioning."

Gregor arose—again startlingly swift for such a large man. He reached the door in a single stride, resumed his foreigner affect. "I have *not* finish confer with my client! From what I've heard thus far, I say with some confidence that we will leaving shortly—no further questioning." He shoved the door shut, the officer narrowly avoiding the loss of his nose. Gregor's shoulders bounced as he silently chuckled.

I went on. "You said 'demon.' Is that the ... I don't know ... *official* term? I mean, among our ... among *us?*" It felt so strange for there to exist an "our kind" or "us." Stranger still to be saying the words aloud. Deeper in my mind, I was uncomfortable with the idea of any sort of affiliation with this man. But at that moment in time all I saw before me was a vast library of knowledge about myself. If he wished to patronize and demean me as a feeble whelp, I would not protest. I had grown more than accustomed to condescension.

"Demon, yes. It is a label I enjoy. There is really no better modern term."

"What about *soul?*" I said. "Are we not simply lost souls? Are you familiar with Empedocles?"

"Soul, if you like." His demeanor had changed. He suddenly appeared weary, bored. He scrawled some notes on his pad and glanced at me. "I must take my leave. Do stay put until after I am well away from the building." He gathered his things back into his briefcase.

"Wait, you're leaving without me? What about me? You told them—"

"It matters not. I told you, you should leave this crooked scum. He was a bad choice to begin with. Come find me when you've acquired new apparel." He knocked on the door and stepped out with a nod to the young officer. "Good day."

The officer appeared as flummoxed as I was. He looked at me. "He leaving?"

I shook my head and shrugged as if I wasn't sure. The door clicked shut as I heard him call out to the detectives.

I had no idea what to do next. Was I actually attached to this body? Gregor's euphemism: *apparel*. Bodies were simply clothing to him. I closed my eyes and let my chin drop to my chest. Did I feel so differently? As much as I wished to believe it, my actions thus far certainly did not suggest it was the case. Unless I somehow died, there would always be a next body. The question before me: was I indeed ready for a new suit? And did I have a choice?

9. Gregor

"Your kraut lawyer comin' back?" Detective Morton asked. "What's going on?"

I stared at him with my best smug face, crossed my arms. "Oh, he'll be back. I told him I don't want to make a big production out of it, but he insisted this could be huge. Something about the city having deep pockets ... ." I watched his gears turning, saw reason battling machismo.

I wondered, *Does this guy truly think I did something?*

I let my hands fall to my lap and spoke earnestly. "I really would rather go home and continue searching for my girlfriend. Yes, I've done bad things in the past, but that was a long time ago. I'm about to earn my Master's degree. I work at a library, for Pete's sake."

"Graduating to white collar, eh? Shit don't stop smelling when you bring it inside."

"I'll not argue against that statement, Detective. And I'll not claim that I was a good man all those years ago."

It looked like I might have gotten through; Morton's dissecting stare appeared less sure than before. "You killed a guy in Kansas."

The window was open! He was inviting me to argue, to convince him!

"That was a fight that got out of hand, and it was an accident." I had no idea of the details around Tinker's manslaughter conviction, and I hoped Morton didn't either. "Six guys in a pileup, Detective. I was just the lucky one they pulled out last. You know I'd still be locked up if it was something more than that. I'd ask you to call my professors and co-workers, but I would hate for them to know the sort of person I used to be ... It's obviously your prerogative, though."

* * *

As I crossed the street away from the precinct, I tried not to be too self-congratulatory. Eileen was still missing and the police would most certainly be keeping a close eye on me. They had a box of deviant, sexual violence-centric contraptions, and the more they looked in there, the more my cleaned-up, back-on-track guise would melt away. Soon they would come knocking on my door, or worse, arrest me at work or school. Where the hell was Eileen? I chided myself with a fresh rush of shame for continuing to entertain the idea that this was all some horrible game to punish me and refocus my attention on her. Such thoughts inevitably gave way to images of her bloated body washing up on the bank of the East River, her skin gray and nibbled. Sometimes she had stab wounds, other flashes had her tied up with rope formerly bound to a massive chunk of concrete. But this lawyer (among other things), Gregor, and the newsstand guy both said they had seen her in the past couple days. I had to believe them and hold onto that knowledge.

And what about this Gregor? How long had he been watching me, or aware of my presence in the city? He hadn't simply happened upon me in the park. My fear and desperation around finding Eileen was mixed with uneasy excitement over the prospect of speaking more with Gregor. How I was supposed to find him? And would it be inappropriate for me to put any focus on tracking him down and learning from him while Eileen's fate remained a mystery? I had to talk to Stan.

I noticed the lack of traffic on the streets and glanced at my watch. Close to midnight. Too late to pop in on Stan so I headed home, my mind a noisy jumble of everything I had to tell him. Stan wouldn't question any of it; it felt good to have someone that *knew*. Well, I supposed now there were two.

I wondered, given this talk of me abandoning my Geoffrey body, would Stan accept me if I did have to escape, showing up at his door one day with a new face? "Hey, Stan, it's me, Samuel—that you knew as Geoff. You can call me Phil now."

I wondered if Gregor's simplistic outlook might just be the most logical. Of course I always knew the "leave" card sat ready in my back pocket, but in his chilling little pig eyes, abandoning a body appeared to require little pre-consideration. Have some trouble? New body! I had never worked that way. I supposed if I did—if I felt no guilt toward the body's true owner—I would be a much happier person.

My current attempt at remorse avoidance (take the body of a low-life criminal) would work beautifully if not for criminal *records*. I had previously considered taking such a body abroad, start fresh in a land with no extradition treaty with the U.S. But I loved my country. I didn't *want* to leave.

A taxi finally appeared up the block and I flagged it down.

"Harlem, East Hundred and Sixteenth, please."

We sped off.

Without guilt holding me back, the ideal home would seem to start in childhood. Perhaps even in infancy, but the idea of being trapped with such limitations for so many years, obliged to *act* every moment of every day until the body's maturity matched the mind's, was not an attractive option. I guessed that Gregor wouldn't think twice to wipe an infant, and probably wouldn't bother acting.

I was curious: why would Gregor use such a strange body? Perhaps the real Gregor Német was rich. And was it just a borrow, or had Gregor wiped the original owner? He seemed to judge me when I revealed that Tinker was gone. There had to be *something* about the body that drew him to it, but then again I knew nothing of this self-described demon. I knew not what motivated him or how he chose his "apparel." And I wanted to know everything about him, and everything he knew of our kind.

* * *

Something was attacking my skull. Screaming, jarring—I tried to roll away from it. I blinked in the suddenly silent darkness of my bedroom. The noise blared again, but now it was only the telephone. I looked at the curtains. No light peeking through. Still nighttime, early morning. How long had I been asleep?

Ring!

Still disoriented, I grappled with the receiver and pressed it to my ear. "Hello?"

"You don't sleep, do you?" I instantly recognized the deep, accented voice.

"Gregor?"

"You know you don't need to."

"I'll try that out that some other night, Gregor. I'm exhausted. Look, can we—"

"Come to my office today. After nine. Német and Sons Attorneys. Ninetieth, just east of Third."

I hung up and collapsed back into bed, my mind freshly abuzz with annoyance and curiosity and questions. I eventually managed a couple more hours of sleep before the invading morning sunlight would have it no more.

I had a plate of eggs and toast with coffee at my corner diner before hopping the subway down to the Upper East Side. Gregor's law office was only a few blocks walk from the station. At six stories, the burgundy building was a tiny brick compared to the adjacent towers. The wall directory guided me to Gregor's suite, #17, on the third floor. Up the linoleum-coated stairs, down a thin hall, I found #16, #18, and a blank brown door between.

I knocked. No answer.

I looked at my watch: 9:34.

I tried again to no avail, pressed my ear to the door, hearing no sounds from inside.

Quick, clicking steps ascended the stairs down the hall. A woman appeared on the floor, daisy-patterned dress with matching hat. She turned my way and came swifting toward me at a determined pace, purse in both hands before her. I couldn't tell if she was someone's client or worked here, but she seemed to know exactly where she was going. She glanced at me as she passed, lips pressed into a polite smile. I smiled in return.

"Good morning," I said as she clicked by. She slowed in front of door #18 and keys jingled into her hands. I began, "Pardon me, ma'am, do you happen to know—" but all I got were wide, suspicious eyes and that same flat smile before she disappeared and shut the door behind her.

I paced.

9:45.

10:01.

I walked downstairs and had a look around at street level. How long would I wait? Ten minutes? Another hour? Where would I go when I decided to give up? Stan was at work by now. I settled on ten minutes, walked upstairs, and sat down against the wall by the door. After a minute passed I heard a heavy rolling sound followed by a deep metal thud, like a filing cabinet being closed. I stood up and knocked on the door. Heavy footsteps on a wooden floor approached and the door swung open. Before me stood a smirking Gregor in a navy blue suit.

"Ah, I was wondering when you would show up. Come in."

"I've been knocking for the past half hour."

"I heard nothing. Come in now, please. We have much to discuss."

Unnerved, I walked into the short hallway, taking in the cluttered space. Overstuffed file boxes lined the walls, bookshelves packed with dusty volumes, the massive filing cabinet I had just heard, a metal desk blanketed with papers, books, and notepads. The only two windows were covered in yellowed newspapers, tinting what little light entered the office. What appeared to be a sloping pile of boxes and chaotic paper stacks against a wall turned out to be a buried couch. Closed doors on both side walls.

Gregor groaned down into his desk chair and gestured to the only other available seat: a wooden bar stool. "Please, make yourself comfortable."

I sat, feeling odd to be so high up in the room, but realizing my eyes rose only slightly higher than his. I still felt on display. Gregor opened and closed drawers behind his desk, mumbling happily and whistling some tune between his teeth.

"You have sons?" I asked to fill the air.

He peeked up at me from behind his desk. "Ah, no. Children inspire in me only confusion and rage."

"So your sign ... The law firm ... ."

"Yes, yes." He waved me off as he settled into his chair. "Lends to legitimacy. Family and the like. *They* like this sort of thing. So you decided to keep that troublesome body."

"Yes."

"How did you manage your way out of the precinct? A game of body hopscotch?"

"No, they released me because they knew I wasn't guilty."

Gregor laughed, moist and throaty. "A likely story! But not to worry, I will prod no further. We must respect each other's unknowns, mustn't we? Such is the nature of our nature, is it not?" He slid a legal pad from beneath a pile, put on a pair of glasses, and scrutinized the top page for a moment. "Hmph." He tore off the first sheet and placed it facedown atop one of his stacks, plucked a thick pen from a coffee mug, and set his eyes back on me. "Let us talk. I ask you a question, you ask me a question. We both answer with all due candor. Back and forth, back and forth. Sounds good?"

It sounded very good. I nodded. He smiled with teeth, like the devil after being handed a freshly signed soul contract. A bad feeling washed over me.

Pen at the ready, he asked, "First, where were you born?"

"California."

"Sure, fine, but perhaps I should say *how* were you born? The circumstances."

I readied my lungs and retold the story of my beginning. Gregor listened and jotted notes. I watched as his considerable nostrils flared with each inhale. I read his demeanor as that of one who had conducted innumerable meetings of this sort.

"...and that was when I realized that my stepfather would never awaken."

"Mmm ... delicious justice. Surprisingly rare in the cases of those whose death was directly caused by another. Disorientation tends to last longer than in your experience. Now, on to—"

A phone rang somewhere behind his desk. He held up a finger and rolled backward. "One moment, please." He leaned over and produced a telephone from some unseen stand—I guessed a box or stack of papers. "Némct and Sons Probate Attorn—ah, yes, hello Ms. Carole ... I understand, though I am with client at the— yes, I understand. I will add to my ... Well, we can't allow to happen, now can we? Of course not ... I will get back to you, Ms. Carole. As I said, I am with client. Good-bye." I heard the woman's desperate voice still jabbering on as Gregor hung up. He sighed, shook his head, and scanned his desk and my face, as if reorienting himself to our conversation. "Apologies. Where were we?"

"I was now going to ask *you* a question."

He leaned back and interlocked his fingers over his belly. "Sure, yes, of course."

"Well, first, I'd like to know the same of you. *Your* story."

"Certainly. Not nearly as scandalous as yours, but I'm happy to share." The phone began to ring again. Gregor glared toward the sound. "Ach, Ms. Carole and your blood money!" He turned back to me. "Just a moment. She'll give up with ten rings." We sat quietly as he held up his fingers: *three, four, five ... eight, nine, ten.* The room fell silent. Gregor smiled. "A hideously bloated divorcee with rich, senile parents. She found out their will had her *only* inheriting a million, and her two daughters splitting another two hundred thousand. What does she do? Manipulates her parents into reducing her own daughters' take to fifteen thousand each. Now she's upset. Not because her last surviving parent died, but because her daughters found out about the altered will and are now suing to have her disinherited all together."

"And you're going to prevent that?"

Gregor laughed. "Absolutely not! I'm the one that informed the daughters! Not only will Ms. Carole soon find herself on welfare, she has forever lost her daughters. She will die poor and alone. All because she wanted an extra fifteen percent." His shoulders quivered as if by a surge of ecstasy.

"Interesting. Now, you were going to share your story with me?"

"Of course. It was the year of their Lord, nine hundred sixty-four. Norway. Some sort of land dispute between neighbors. Three were killed, a father and son from one family, one man from the other. I do not know which one I was, and truly only briefly cared. *Our* lives, you know, begin *after* we *pyoopit*."

"*Pyoopit?*"

"Yes, like an insect. The butterfly from the caterpillar. Our first human shells are our larvae, and should be given as much consideration. Now, back to you. What is it that *drives* you? What it is you *want* out of your existence?"

I couldn't say "love." I was beginning to realize there were many things I didn't want him to know about me. And why did he care so much about this information? Did he create a file on every one of us he encountered, now boxed and stacked against his walls? However, I did need the rest of my own questions answered.

"To learn. To continue learning everything there is to know about ... us."

"Hm." He seemed dissatisfied by my answer—that look of tedium from the police station. "Well, I suppose I'm satisfying your entire life's purpose over the next hour, rendering the rest of it meaningless."

I disregarded his comment. "Before, you said 'year of *their* Lord.' Do you worship a different God?"

He tilted his head and looked at me as if I had instead asked about Santa Claus, his unsettling eyes studying me.

He crossed his arms and finally spoke. "No."

"No you do not worship another, or ... do you not believe in God at all?"

"I answered your question. Now, tell me about your relationship with Eileen. What do you feel you gain from it?"

"I don't know ... What difference does it make? What does anyone gain from any relationship? Same as anyone else." I wanted to find out how he knew Eileen at all, but that would have to come later.

He regarded me. "Is that so?" More notes scribbled on his pad, he narrated as he wrote, "Same ... as .... anyone .... *else.*"

"My turn. What is there about our kind that I don't know?"

He stammered for a beat. "Well, I ... I don't know what you don't know. Probably hundreds of things. And that is not a single question."

"Very well. What is the most important thing about us that I *wouldn't* know?"

"Ah, well put. I would have to say it is the fact that we are not immortal."

I was floored. "We can *die?*"

"I believe that is the definition of mortality. How many bodies have you used since birth? Not including your original."

I blurted, "How can we die? What happens?"

"It is not your turn."

"It doesn't matter! I ... I'll answer what you want, just tell me this one. How can it happen?"

He re-crossed his arms and sat silent.

"Fine! What was the question? How many bodies?" I counted in my head to be sure. Grant Beauchamp, Rip, Aaron Fuller, Jerome Johns, Anton, Vernon, Tinker, Chuck—the vagrant in the library, Wilma—the old lady that was lost. I asked, "Used at all, for any amount of time?"

"If the number is countable."

"Nine. I believe nine."

Gregor frowned as he considered. "Twenty-seven years, nine bodies? That would average to switching every three years."

"Well, a few of those were just borrows. Some only a couple minutes, really. There were actually a couple more of those, a day or two at a time. I don't remember them."

"So your goal is to remain, what, for a decade? A lifetime, allowing conditions?"

I ignored his follow-up. "My question is: how can we die?"

His eyebrow flicked touché. "It does not happen by accident. It is a skill that must be practiced, and very few have ever succeeded. One begins by entering another demon's acquired body, while not allowing them to leave. I would not recommend attempting it. The stronger will always win, regardless of who entered whose body."

"And have you done it? Killed another demon? What happens to them after? How do you know they're truly gone?"

"It is not your turn, but I have an answer. You know they are gone, because you have *torn* them to shreds, and *felt* them perish. It is probably much like what you did to poor Mr. Cuion, only with much more time and effort. This should answer more than one of your *extra* questions. Now tell me, is it your intention to remain in a body for as long as circumstances allow?"

"I suppose so. I wish to live a normal life ... *lives*, I guess."

Gregor tented his fingers before him and strummed the tips, a smile slowly broadening. "I see."

I was afraid of whatever conclusion he had drawn, what it all meant to him, but I couldn't stop. I needed to know about Eileen. It was clear there were endless things he knew that I didn't, and who knew how much he would tell me? Not much, I guessed, if it didn't serve him in some way.

"I must ask you something now," I said. "I hope that you will continue to be honest." His expression did not change. "Did you have anything to do with Eileen's disappearance?"

No hesitation. "Yes."

I was dumbstruck. I had thought he'd known something more, but I hadn't actually expected him to admit anything, or if he had, what I would say or do. All I could say then was, "You did?"

He repeated, "Yes."

I stood up. "What did you ... I mean, where is she? Is she okay? What did you do to her?"

"I answered your question. My turn." He peered down through his glasses to the notepad, as if nothing of consequence had just been said. "What demonic skills have you developed thus far?"

I spoke through my teeth. "I am not answering any more questions until you answer mine. What have you done with her?"

"Then this would be what they call a *stalemit*. If you answer my question, I will answer yours. It is really quite simple. You may also wish to refer back to your former question and my answers as you stand there in an oh-so-threatening pose. Such physical displays are really for *them*, as admirable an impersonation you've got there, in your red-painted little costume ... ."

I tried to slow my breath, relax my muscles. I was like a shrimp standing up to a whale. It was surely a comical display for him, but my blood was still pulsing in my temples as I sat back down on the stool, quiet.

"Did you need for me to repeat the question, Samuel?"

I swallowed and labored over the words. "Skills ... I don't know what you mean exactly."

"For instance, you surely have mastered the basics of navigation in your true form, choosing to disregard or to interact with an object."

"As in the ground and walls and such, sure." But a moment after I said it, I realized what he had actually revealed. The same method I used for staying above ground, or ascending stairs, applied to other physical objects. Of course it did, but I had never given it much thought beyond what was needed for moving around. I would have to practice this "interaction skill" as well as continue encouraging him to elaborate on his questions. They could be more informative than his answers to mine. Gregor nodded for me to go on. "What other things ... It's difficult to identify, you know, when things become second nature ... perhaps if you list—?"

"Of course you would enjoy that, but this is not demon training class."

"Well then assume I don't have any special skills beyond what I guess are the basics. I don't know anything. I'm just a baby, like you said."

"So nothing with hosts besides taking them, eh?"

"Such as?"

He waved off the question, scrawled more notes.

The Many Lives of Samuel Beauchamp

What did it mean, "nothing with hosts?" What else could be done with them? Back to Eileen...

I said, "My turn?" He gestured for me to proceed. I framed my question as best as I could. "What was your involvement in Eileen's disappearance, and what is her current status?"

"Again, two questions. One, I am not the reason Ms. Scoville left, but I definitely incited her departure."

"How? You didn't answer the question. The question was how."

His hands bounced a settle down motion. "I wasn't done. I incited her departure ... by telling her what you are."

Michael Siemsen

10. Where D'ye Hyde?

Gregor had claimed he told Eileen what I was. If it was true, then she obviously believed him and went into hiding, not even packing her things before running. It would certainly be the first reasonable explanation for why she would have left in such a hurry. But why would she believe it? Eileen was the most skeptical, dismissive person I'd known when it came to anything supernatural. She didn't even believe in God.

I recalled the time we had walked past the crowded steps of a Lutheran church on a Sunday morning, a delighted woman in pink waving a flyer at us. "You won't find the *Word* down that way, my friends. Jesus—" Eileen had interrupted her by suggesting an incestuous, paradoxical explanation for the Immaculate Conception. I had hurried Eileen away from the speechless group, and asked her if she had any fear of going to hell.

"The only hell I believe in is inside that fucking church back there."

I found myself once more on my feet in front of Gregor's cluttered desk. "What exactly did you tell her?" He rolled his thumbs around each other in a circle. "And *why?* Why would you possibly tell her anything about me?"

He leaned forward and placed his elbows on the desk. "So simple. I told her for the same reason I called the police and told them to look into Kansas. To *help* you. You must release yourself from this prison."

"*Help?* You've ruined my life!" I strode to the door and turned back. "You need to stay away from me. I swear to God!"

"That is adorable," he said. "I promise I won't make any more calls."

Restraining my rage, I twisted the knob and then paused. I looked back once more.

"Did you say anything to anyone else?"

A faux-apologetic grin curled into his cheeks and he turned up his hands. "Sorry."

I took a step back and shouted. "Who?"

"I may have let slip your Kansas troubles to a Mr. McGeorge at the library."

"My boss? What is your problem? What do you care about my life?"

"...perhaps a professor or two... a lad named Donald at the library, your friend Stanley..."

I stormed out and slammed the door behind me.

I found a phone booth down the street and called the library. The assistant director, Don, answered.

"Hi, Don, this is Geoff. I just wanted to let you all know I'm not feeling well today, so—"

"Nevermind it, Geoff. The director and I were ... talking. We, er, realized we're a bit overstaffed. We're letting you go."

"Don, listen, if this is about—"

He interrupted, "Sorry, Geoff," and hung up.

It was true. Gregor had gotten to everyone in my life that mattered. My job was gone. My Masters was likely at risk. My girlfriend was in hiding (a relief to some degree, knowing she was likely not in danger). Fortunately for me, his intrusion would not work on Stan. I hopped the subway to midtown where Stan worked at the Metropolitan Club. Inside the heavy door, a large tuxedoed man at a lectern held his hand up to me.

"Members only, sir."

"Right, I'm just here to ... ." I stopped myself, not wanting to get Stan in trouble. "Could I just use the restroom? I'll be quick."

"Most certainly not."

I peered around him but couldn't see past the horizon of polished darkwood stairs.

"You need to leave."

I walked out, defeated.

Exasperation began turning to manic desperation. I stood at the corner of the busy street, the frenzied intersection of grumbling trucks and cars reflecting the chaos in my head. I needed to get away, someplace quiet. I wanted to leave Tinker's body behind once and for all, but what had once been a commitment to myself had shifted to an act of stubborn defiance. Why must it be that I meet for the first time another of my kind, and he, too, wants to push me around like everyone else?

Now, there was only Stan. Calm, carefree Stan that Gregor thought he could flush from my world like the others. I sighed and returned to the tunnels below ground, took the train to Stan's. In case the police were watching Eileen's building, I walked the alley to the back entrance, past the rotting smell of the dumpsters. I let myself into Stan's apartment with the hidden key, guzzled water from the tap, and lay down on the long cozy couch. It felt so good to be off my feet in his quiet living room, the buzz of the city below reduced to a calming hum.

I fell asleep.

* * *

I awoke to a sudden smack to my face. I found the weapon on the floor beside the couch: a tasseled throw pillow.

"You scared the devil out of me," Stan said with a wink. "So to speak."

"Oh, Stan." I sat up and wiped my face with both hands. "You're not going to believe what's happened."

He tossed his keys on the kitchen bar. "Something to do with your weird friend, I'm thinking?"

"Oh, God. Did he come here?"

"Yeah, woke me up this morning. Wouldn't stop knocking. So what's happening? He said you were in some sort of danger?"

I glanced outside, noted the darkening sky. I'd been asleep for hours. "He said that? Danger? Well, yes, but what else did he say?"

"Just that he needed to find you. Warn you about someone."

"Wait, what did this man look like?"

"Nondescript, I suppose. Handsome sort. Like a silver-haired William Holden."

"That is not who I was thinking of. What else did he say?"

"That's all. Danger, needs to find you, had been to your place. I called you right after he left, but it was early. I figured you were still counting sheep."

Who could it have been? Police having second thoughts? Neither of the detectives matched Stan's description, and they would have found me at home. And who would they be warning me about?

Stan grabbed two bottles of pop from the refrigerator, put one in my hand, and sat down beside me on the couch.

"So fill me in, buddy. What's going on?"

I relayed the whole tale to Stan, starting with Gregor in the park, the police in front of my apartment, the station, and then my meeting at Gregor's office. "Now, he said he spoke with you on the phone, thought he was revealing my secrets to you, along with everyone else that knows me."

"Not me. Maybe he called the wrong number. Some other Stan's out there thinkin' 'who the heck is Geoff?' Kind of funny."

"Not really. Well, I'm almost certain he spoke with the management at the library. Why else would they suddenly fire me?"

"I don't know, but I'd sure try to stay away from this guy. You believe he's really ... you know, *like you?*"

"One-hundred percent. He knows everything, and much more. More than me, at least. I believe he's been around for a very long time."

"Well, it sure sounded like the silver-haired guy wants to help you."

"Did he give a name? Say how I could reach him?"

Stan grimaced. "Dang it, it was awful early. He said a name, but ... ." He tried to remember but shook his head. "Bill? Jim? Nope. Gone. But he said he would keep trying to find you. I think your best bet is your place, long as the coppers don't come knocking again."

"I think you're right." I stood up. "Would it be too much trouble for you to come with? I hate to ask."

"Ah, buddy. You know I would, but—"

I waved him off. I shouldn't have asked. "Forget about it, really. I forgot." He had his second job on Tuesday through Thursday nights—overnight security guard at a big bank. He'd been hoping to parlay it into a full-time gig. "I'll be all right."

"You better be. You missed *Peter Gunn* and *Wells* this week."

I smiled. With everything else seeming to crumble, there was always Stan to lighten the mood. "Hey, thanks." I reached out to shake his hand.

He looked at it with a curious smile, then shrugged awkwardly and grasped. "Hey, if the cops come asking me about Eileen, you want I should tell them what a whacko she is? The pills and stuff?" His hand began to slide away, but suddenly re-gripped mine, tight. I looked up at his face and saw a strange expression he'd never worn.

"Well ... Stan?"

A different voice came from his mouth, cruel and mocking. "Yes, and you want I should tell them how you beat her up sometimes? How you insisted upon sodomy? The tears you laughed at and her growing fear of you?"

Gregor! Not Stan ... No ... .

I tried to pull away but his grip tightened. "Let go!"

I yanked my hand away and backed against the door. Stan tripped backward and his face returned to normal, then confused.

"Whoa. Dizzy. So yay or nay on the cops? Just gimme the word. Otherwise I'm just going to tell 'em you're a great guy, wouldn't hurt a fly. You know, all that bullshit."

I needed to leave. Gregor was surely still in the room. The only way to protect Stan was to get away from him.

"Sure, Stan. Gotta go." I slipped out the door, felt the sweat glazing over my forehead. Was Gregor following? My neck felt like an executioner's axe was about to fall on it. I glanced back, as if there were anything to see.

Stan called after me. "You all right, buddy?"

I threw up a curt wave as I cornered out of his sight and down the stairs. On the street, I hailed a taxi.

"Where to?" the driver said, his inquiring eyes in the mirror.

"Hundred and Eleventh and Second, please."

As he drove, I watched the cabby in the rearview mirror, waiting for those eyes to change. He glanced at me here and there, but didn't say anything. Was Gregor in the car? I tried to guess what he was doing—what his goal might be. If indeed he was trying to convince me to shed Tinker's body, to be "free" and unattached to my human "attire," then this was one persuasive method to drive home the point. The only way to get away from him would be to leave the body, run away naked.

I had the driver drop me on the corner near my apartment. For some reason I thought walking half a block might somehow aid my escape from a possibly pursuing Gregor. I stopped in front of my neighborhood diner, watched the faces of pedestrians. No one seemed to take any more notice of me than usual.

I went inside, ordered a cup of coffee and slice of pie. Nothing out of the ordinary transpired. And then I realized the true pointlessness of my actions. Of course Gregor knew where I lived! And if he didn't want me to know he was near, I wouldn't. He had all the power in this situation, and at the moment, I was helpless to prevent anything.

I paid the check, grabbed my hat, and walked to my building. On the steps I found a man in a beige fedora. He looked up at me at once, eyes alert and searching.

"Mr. Cuion?"

I stopped in front of him. "Who are you?"

He was soft spoken, with what sounded to me like a Scottish accent. "My name is Bryn." He stood up, looked both ways down the street. "We need to talk. Do you mind?" He pulled off his hat, gestured with it to the entrance. I observed his silver hair.

"Are you the one that spoke to my friend, Stan?" He nodded. "Is this," I lowered my voice, as if it might summon him, *"Is this about Gregor?"* He nodded again, his face grim, and swung open the door.

* * *

"Your mistake was in changing bodies," Bryn said, his intense eyes boring into mine. He had a strong chin with a deep cleft. I could see Stan's William Holden comparison. Tall, silver haired, broad shouldered, Bryn was indeed a handsome man. "You need to handle that business somewhere far away *before* moving to a new home. He can sense the transition and then find you by your corona. But it's too late. You're already in his sights. You need to—"

I interrupted, "Sorry, Bryn, but who are you? I see you're trying to help me, but as you might imagine, I'm a bit shell-shocked at present. How did *you* find me? How do you know Gregor? Why would—"

"I know. There isn't much magnanimity among our kind. It is because of monsters like him. But there are good ones out there. Until you are stronger it is best you keep moving and blend, but do not grow so jaded from your experience with him that you avoid us all together." He leaned back in my chair and crossed his legs. "You want to know about me? Who I am?" I nodded. "I'm American, originally. Late eighteenth century. I was in the exact position you're in now, but not a week old. Gregor appeared, acted like he was going to take me under his wing."

"Sorry," I said, suddenly paranoid again. "But how do we know he's not here now?"

"Well, I would see him."

"You can see a free-roaming demon?"

"I don't use that word. But yes. Not with the eyes, mind you ... ." He stopped, waved his hands. "We don't have time for that right now. I'll teach you what I can later. Just know for now that the only way to hide is in a body, and you have to pull your corona in."

"What's a corona?"

He waved me off again. "Later. As I was saying, Gregor came to me a shortly after my beginning. Camden, South Carolina.

He was an ensign serving under Cornwallis, battling the colonies. I knew next to nothing at the time and he taught me quite a lot. Had me take over one of his lieutenants, and we continued on with the British Army. I discovered what he *really* was when I refused to take Lord Cornwallis. Gregor went into fits—how dare I not follow his every direction? He stabbed me, forced me to take another body, killed him, too. Before he cut the throat of the third, he told me 'this only stops when baby learns to listen to Daddy.'"

"So did you? Go into the British General?"

"No. I left the area without a body. Traveled north for a week before borrowing a sailor shipping out back to England. I've lived there since, and fortunately he hasn't come calling."

"Wow. Well, congratulations. I suppose that's what you're going to tell me to do? Flee the country?"

He shook his head. "No. I wasn't with him long enough for his obsession with me to grow. Since he dug his roots in New York, however, he's found and targeted more than a dozen. And that's just the ones I'm aware of. Those before you ... I saw it first hand—it's terrifying."

"How?" I asked. "How do you see all this from England? How did you know about me?"

"I stop in every so often. Try to help those in his sights. Sometimes it works ... ." My eyes drifted off as the weight on my shoulders grew heavier. Bryn waited a moment before going on. "Now, just to give you a bit more of an idea," he searched his coat pockets, plucking out an old, wrinkled paper, "of what you're dealing with. Read this."

I unfolded the sheet and saw that it had been torn from a book. The page header read SUPERSTICIONS of CAVERSHAM ~ *Charms*. I skimmed past an introductory paragraph to a passage circled in blue ink.

Gregyr Gregyr, where d'ye hyde?
Eldshire forest, on th'other syde.
Long its been since last ye stayd
Fear ye not, but be ye 'frayd
Who shall ye choose, duiell, next time round?
An olde widow seem a pick well found.
Pray thee shall and work thyn hand
lest ye join myne cursed clan.

"When is this from?" I asked.

"The book was published in the late nineteenth century, but it's compiled from earlier volumes. That rhyme in particular dates back to the twelfth century."

My eyes floated over the words again. "I wonder if he knows about it."

"Are you kidding? This is his pride and joy. It's the reason he still uses that name. He terrorized that village for three centuries, often waiting several years, then snatching someone when the people began to relax and forget, or just when the young children of the next generation began to question the legend. You should see how his eyes light up when this charm is mentioned. But don't speak of it. He'll know I'm here."

I read it once more, regarded Bryn as he squeezed his meaty fists and incessantly cracked his knuckles. The man was intense, humorless. It made Gregor seem all the more frightening to me, the gravity with which Bryn spoke of him.

"His entire world is his game, and you are now his favorite player."

"Why are you helping me? If this puts you at risk, what do you get out of it?"

"Because I know what it's like to be his project. Like I said, not to the extreme of this focus he seems to have on you. But even though I hadn't been around as long as you, there was something different about me. For all his power, he couldn't get in my head and snoop around, couldn't push me out—"

"Wait, what do you mean? Can he get in my head?"

A grave nod. "I'm certain he already has. See, we're all a little different. I don't know you all that well, but I can see where you're weak. Until you're more aware and skilled, you're vulnerable to any number of invasions. If his focus right now is to get you to abandon that body, he will eventually push you out, take it from you, and kill it while you watch. Don't worry right away though. This is the most patient individual you will ever meet. Existing for thousands of years tends to skew the experience of time."

"*Thousands* of years? He said he was coming up on one thousand."

"It should have been obvious to you by now, but don't believe anything he says."

"Thousands ... ." I tried to imagine what that must be like, watching the world change before your eyes. Life must move exceptionally slow to an immortal. "Think of the madness that must go on in his mind. Do you think he's simply bored? Do you think by now ... I don't know, perhaps he longs for death?"

My question seemed to catch Bryn off-guard. "Bored? No. And do not think for an instant that he is insane! This being is the sharpest intellect you will ever encounter. Listen to me, Samuel. I'm going to teach you what I can in as little time as possible, but it's important while we're doing so that you remain in that body. As long as you don't switch bodies, he can't track you. If you must, do so out of the state. There are reasons he chose Manhattan for home, and those are size and density. Understand? He can sense an entry from miles away, and there are remnants ... signs when a body's been used. They leave a trail, even after you leave them. He'll track backwards to you if you're not careful. That's surely how he found you in the first place. And with your corona flaring out like that ... well, it wasn't difficult for him."

I wondered how long I had been in Gregor's sights. The last time I'd taken a body was six months before—a confused old lady wandering through the busy street in front of the library. It must have set off some alarm. I felt sick at the idea that he had invaded my head, as Bryn suggested, eavesdropping on any number of private thoughts and moments. He could know *everything* about my relationship with Eileen.

Something occurred to me. Eileen was in hiding, not dead or in danger. I was out of a job, my Masters had surely been sabotaged. Besides Stan, who was now in peril thanks to me, what was keeping me in the city? Gregor wanted me to leave this body, and I wondered why I wouldn't simply go a step further and leave the city entirely. I had no interest in playing his game, or some vain attempt to resist him.

"Bryn," I said. "Should I just leave? Like you did?"

"Well ... I suppose it comes down to your relationships—how much you value them. I had no such ties when I fled to sea. There's your girlfriend to consider. Your friend, Stanley. I do not know you well enough to advise, but you seem a decent enough fellow. Think on what's most important to you."

"I think both would be better off without me in their lives. It would be selfish of me to remain."

Bryn only held his gaze, an expression of neither approval nor objection. "Either way, let's get you up to speed tonight. Meet me at this address. Ten o'clock, and stay away from any of your usual haunts, so to speak." He handed me a scrap of paper.

I killed time by heading to the Seward Park Library in the Lower East Side, about as far from my place as I could get without actually leaving Manhattan. I tried to keep my corona "in" as much as possible, while having no idea if what I was doing made any difference at all. This would be one of the most important things Bryn would teach me. Likewise the ability to spot signs of other daimons.

At the library, I tried to find a copy of the book from which Gregor's rhyme had been torn, *Supersticions of Caversham*, but of course they didn't have anything remotely similar.

* * *

In the evening, I pulled Bryn's scrap of paper from my pocket. The address led me to a brick factory building in the Garment District. I found Bryn waiting inside a vast warehouse area with cables hanging over an endless row of metal tables.

"Let's move to a smaller area," he said and I followed him to a room off the main factory floor. A sign hung outside the door, the number 2 written in chalk:

2 DAYS since last accident
Mind Your Fingers, Hair, and Clothing

Beyond the door was a windowless meeting room with cinderblock walls and a single fluorescent light over a long table. Bryn closed his eyes and stood in silence for a moment. "We're clear ... for now." We moved a long table to the side of the room and stacked the chairs out of the way.

Bryn didn't teach me as much as I had hoped, but what he did show me would later prove invaluable. All my life, apparently, I had been walking around with a big "DAIMON" sign across my body. Bryn taught me to spot others by their unique corona, the visible aura or waves that emanate from every person. You have to be looking for it, but I found that even from across a street, a daimon's corona extends farther than regular people, and is drawn to passers-by, whereas most human waves appear indifferent to those around them. We went out onto 7th Avenue and I watched as Bryn let his corona go, demonstrating the effect for me as he strolled past a cluster of women sifting through fruit baskets outside the market. Threads of distorted light stretched out from his body and caressed others' waves in passing.

Back at the factory, he taught me how to pull mine in, much like sucking in one's gut. Fortunately, the strings do not actually produce any light themselves, and are therefore only visible in the daytime or in lit locales. We practiced until he thought I had it down.

Next, he taught me to do the opposite: stretch out as far as possible. This was the method he used for finding any bodiless daimons in a room. Bryn left his body outside the door. My goal was to find where he was hiding in the room, or determine that I was actually alone. It was difficult for me to sustain, but Bryn said it was like stretching any muscle. My elasticity would increase with practice. For now, I just had to walk around the room to cover all ground.

I asked, "How do I get in another's head?" but received wary scrutiny in return.

"That's an offensive tool. You need to focus on defense."

I nodded. "So, is this it then?"

"No, you need to learn how to get out of Gregor's game. If you run and hide, the game simply changes to hunting you down. If you remain and try to ignore him, live your life, he'll enjoy destroying your world."

"He's already done that."

"Not quite. I fear he's only just begun with you."

I sat down on a stack of chairs. "So what do I do?"

"Well, if you play into it, do what he wants—always reluctantly—he might just grow bored with you and move on. It's happened before. Just don't do anything to provoke him."

"Or?"

Bryn thought for a moment, then turned back to me with hesitant eyes. "Or you could join him. Offer to be his apprentice. He'd like that. Tell him you'll do whatever he wants, that you just want to learn from him."

Whoa ...

"I don't think I could do that."

"You asked for an alternative. It would definitely win you some new skills. Things even I don't know how to do."

"And when I can't stand it anymore, how do I get away then?"

Bryn shrugged. "Make it a condition up front. 'I'll work for you, but when I'm done, you let me go with no strings attached.' He might put some conditions on it, but to earn true freedom from him? That's priceless. I'm just sorry I haven't thought of it before." He stared at the blank wall, perhaps recalling those he had previously tried to help escape Gregor.

"If I just run ... just leave the state, the country even, what are my chances of keeping clear of him? If he likes Manhattan so much, why would he bother coming after me?"

Bryn's expression remained grim. He looked in my eyes for a moment before replying, "The game will always be more important than the field."

Michael Siemsen

11. Danger

I knocked on Stan's apartment door. He usually slept in on Saturdays, but not past 9:00, and it was nearly 10:00. A few seconds later, I heard a crash from down the hall, toward Eileen's place. I ran down the hall and pressed my ear to her door. Nothing. I knocked.

"Eileen?" I shouted. "Eileen, are you in there? You need to ... I'd really love to talk to you."

Still no sounds from her apartment, but just as I was about to give up I heard loud footsteps across a hardwood floor behind me. I glanced back and saw the door to 4B. I wasn't sure who lived there, never seen anyone come or go. I stepped across the hall and knocked on the door. Hushed voices. A door closing. The squeaking of old floorboards as someone else, someone *without* heavy shoes, approached the door. They stopped right on the other side. I looked at the peephole just as the light on the side of it was cut off by someone's head. A brief pause. Rattling of chain, retracting deadbolt, the door opened a crack, and I saw the sweat-glazed face of a large colored man nearly a foot taller than me. His body blocked any view into the apartment.

"The fuck you want, four-eyes?" he said.

I swallowed and stammered. "I was just, maybe you know ..." I sucked in a breath and pointed behind me. "Do you happen to know Eileen, the woman that lives next door?"

The man produced a lit cigarette from behind the door, wrapped his lips around the end as he eyed me. The smoke blew out his nose and mouth as he finally replied.

"Yeah, I might'a knowed her." His posture relaxed subtly. "Once or twice." A tobacco-stained grin spread across his face.

It stung the moment he said it. I looked down at the floor, saw a bare foot sticking out the door. He was the man she'd been with when I walked in that night, sprawled on his back across her bed.

But it was a minor revelation, I told myself, shutting away the disturbing visions. And he may actually know something. No need for *those* images to reenter my brain.

"Lovely. Listen, have you seen her around lately? As in, the past week?"

He shook his head, pitying. "Man, what you care for? She's ain't wanna see your white ass." He pulled the door open wider and leaned out toward me. "She found her some more filling meat." He chuckled.

I glanced between his arm and body and observed someone else in the apartment. They were seated in a high-backed chair, legs resting on an ottoman.

"Look, I just need to speak with her. Is she here? Is she inside?"

"Nah, man, she ain't here. Get the fuck on." He stepped back in and slammed the door.

Deadbolt locked, chain secured, floorboards squeaking away.

Asshole.

I walked back toward Stan's place and had an idea. I could have Stan watch over my body while I checked out the neighbor's place. Even if she wasn't there, the guy was hiding something. At the very least, he knew more than he'd let on. I wondered if the police had bothered questioning him. Probably not.

Stan opened his door a few seconds after I knocked.

"Hey, buddy."

I stepped inside. "Sorry to wake you. I really need to talk to you."

"Oh I wasn't asleep. Just reading the paper. You hear about Jack Parr? He's leaving the Tonight Show!"

"Huh, whaddya know." I guessed he hadn't heard my earlier knock. "Listen ... ." and then I remembered the last time I had stood in that spot in Stan's apartment. Gregor had entered him, threatened me—and by the very act of possession, threatened Stan. He could have been in that room, just waiting for his next play. "Hang on a second," I said, and closed my eyes.

I stretched myself out thin, like Bryn had taught me, letting my "corona" ooze down, concentrating around my ankles. It felt somewhat like wetting one's pants. From there, the thin tentacles, like animated lengths of tattered twine, slithered out as far as I could reach them, curling in and around furniture and up walls. As far as I could tell, the room was clear, but I didn't trust my skills enough to be confident. I wouldn't be mentioning my real plans or Bryn's name, just in case. I opened my eyes. Stan appeared amused.

"Reefer?"

"What? No! I was just ... seeing something."

"A daimon thing, huh? You learn some new stuff you haven't told me about? Do share."

"Look, it doesn't matter right now. Listen, I might not be around for a while. I have to go places ... do some things."

"You might want to be vaguer. I'm getting overwhelmed with specifics over here."

"You'll have to trust me, Stan. There's a reason I'm not sharing details. I can't let anything happen to you."

Stan's face appeared more annoyed than intrigued or concerned. "So that's it? You're not even going to tell me the *city* you're going to? What if I don't hear back from you and want to track you down? And why are you running away anyway? If you didn't do anything wrong, you have nothing to hide or run from." He shook his head. "Trust you. Huh. Right."

"Stan—"

"I mean *did* you do something? What aren't you telling me? He doesn't trust you anymore ... ." Stan's voice and expression had flipped like a switch. A smile he'd never made spread into his cheeks. "Know what he's thinking right now? He's thinking maybe you had something to do with his wife after all. Such a sad person, this Stan. Think I'll do him a favor."

"Leave him alone, Gregor! What do you want? Just tell me what it is you want!"

He smiled wider, and then Stan returned, shook out his head, and surveyed his surroundings. He gave me an odd, curious look and then said, "Stay here a minute. I need to check on something."

Stan turned around and walked across his living room to the large street-facing window. He slid it open and climbed out to the metal fire escape.

I rushed after him. "Stan? What are you doing? What could you possibly be checking out there?"

"Just settle down!" He was suddenly over-the-top angry. "This'll only take a second!" And then he eased over the handrail to the outside of the fire escape, nothing between his body and the concrete below but three stories of air. He peered down, rolled his shoulders, and pushed off.

* * *

Stan sustained a few scrapes and bruises. He fought with me, arguing, as I wrestled him back over the rail and through the window. He had truly believed there was a critical thing in need of his "checking" somewhere between the fourth floor and the ground.

I straddled him and held his shoulders on the floor behind his recliner until he calmed down.

"What do you think I'm gonna do?" he yelled.

"You're not going out there again, Stan."

"What, you think I was gonna jump or something? I wasn't going to jump. I'm not crazy, you know."

I eased off his shoulders and leaned back.

"Now get the hell off me."

I got up and closed the window, stood in front of it.

"I think you need to leave, Geoff. You got all these secrets and I'm not friend enough for you to tell. Just go."

"Stan, I don't think you're thinking straight right now, but just know I'm only trying to protect—"

"My fucking hero." He plopped down onto the couch.

I didn't know how or what exactly Gregor had done to him, but Stan was *not* acting anything like himself. It seemed as though Gregor had deposited some false memory or objective in Stan's head. With that kind of power he could devastate any life he wanted, and wouldn't even have to be there to see it through. I decided once and for all that this would be the last time I saw Stan, and this conviction set a painful lump in my throat.

I opened the door and glanced back. He was still on the couch, fuming toward the coffee table.

I'm sorry, Stan.

I closed the door behind me.

A few steps down the hall something hit me. Gregor had surely been there the whole time. He had jumped in Stan, dropped his suicidal action plan in, then popped out and sat back to watch the entertainment. It also meant that he would be following me to wherever I went next. So how to escape?

I continued walking down the hall toward the stairway.

As I approached the stairway, it occurred to me that for all of Gregor's dismissal of and contempt toward committing to a single body, he had certainly been faithful thus far to his strange, lanky form. And of all the bodies to occupy! There's a question I should have asked him during our exchange: "So why the horrible body?"

188

Descending the stairs, I felt an eerie chill run up my spine and around my neck—the sensation of knowing something invisible lurks behind you. I stopped at the second floor, no longer able to stand the feeling, and sent out my "tentacles" again.

If he had been following me, he must have left quickly. I could detect no sign of him, at least not close by. I didn't know why that made me feel better.

I rounded the corner to the next flight of stairs, then down the last set to the lobby doors. Just then, one of the doors swung open and in walked another level of eerie.

"Geoffrey?" An unkempt Eileen gawked up at me in horror. She dropped the bag she was carrying and brought both hands around her belly. Her slightly protruding, abnormally round belly.

My initial reaction to seeing her face (the desire to engage in uncharacteristic violence) vanished, replaced by a million racing thoughts. Relief that she was alive, wanting to grab hold of her wrist and march her into the nearest police precinct, rage at the past, curiosity and fear about this apparent pregnancy, shame, guilt, confusion. She had only been missing for a couple weeks. Standing before me there, she must have been showing three or four months along. But how did I not notice it earlier? Had she been hiding it? Had she known?

I stammered, "You're ... You have a—"

"I tried to tell you. But that doesn't matter now. Please just let me by and stay away from me."

"Eileen, hang on." I put up a hand and she recoiled as if it were a gun. "Look, I'm not going to hurt you, if that's what you think. When have I ever ... ."

"Please, Ge—whatever your name is—just let me by. I only need to get a few things and you'll never see me or your child again."

"Your? My?" I stepped off the final step to her level. I looked at her belly. "How do you know... I mean, are you sure that it's ... ."

Her expression of fear finally changed to one I knew all too well: supreme irritation. But it only served to reset my perception of her to where it should always remain.

"It's a reasonable question," I said. "We both know it is."

"It's yours, fuckwad! I'm at four months. Your fragile little cock was somehow still enough for me at that point."

I closed my eyes, simultaneously pushing away images of strangling her, and beset with emotions about the baby inside her. How miserable a life would a mother like her give a child ... *my child*, if I was to believe her, and I did. Her claim of four months did match up with estimation, and looking back to that period, our relationship—such as it was—had been essentially stable, by our standards.

"Well?" she demanded.

"Well, what?" It occurred to me that after I offended her, she had no longer sought to get past me and upstairs. She was waiting for my reaction. The reaction of someone she supposedly feared. If you truly feared someone, would you insult them and call them names? And who exactly did she fear? Samuel the Demon, or Tinker the Murderer? Gregor had claimed he told her what I was, but he had lied about telling Stan things, as well.

"Never mind," she said with melodramatic despondency, and scurried past me to the stairs. "Maybe I'll get rid of it after all."

It *almost* worked. I nearly fell right back into her trap, but— and I'm not ashamed to say I'm proud of myself for that moment— I tipped my hat to her and said, "Have a wonderful life, Eileen." And I walked out the glass doors to the street.

Michael Siemsen

12. The Lair

Looking back, it is difficult to decide whether, in the bigger picture, what happened next was a good thing or bad. I could have left town, disappeared, wondered what might have been. Instead, I stopped three steps down the sidewalk, looked up the brick face of Eileen and Stan's building, and turned around. I didn't know precisely why, but until that moment I had felt that I'd always been on the defensive with everyone in my life—an unwilling or willing participant in someone else's plans or desires, a victim of their mood, prey in their game. I had no plan, but I was going back into those doors.

In the lobby, I hurriedly removed my shoes. I could hear Eileen's footsteps still echoing through the stairwell. I wished there was some closet or crawlspace where I could hide my body, but I still remembered Bryn's warning not to switch bodies. I didn't know if the simple act of leaving my body would set off some alarm in Gregor's head, or if it was only the act of entering a new one. Gregor ... I wondered where he had gone.

Oh God.

If he was still upstairs and spotted Eileen, I didn't think he could resist the urge to do something with her.

Silently ascending three steps at a time, I reached the fourth floor just as Eileen made it to the end of her hall. I heard her keys jingle and slide into the lock. I peered around the corner to see that she was all the way in before I proceeded, but she wasn't at *her* door. She was at the door across from her. The apartment of the colored man I'd earlier had the displeasure of meeting. It was beginning to make sense. Actually, I wasn't sure it did, but something seemed to be coming together in the back of my mind. I felt like I almost had it. It felt as though I just needed a tiny bit more—some small clue—and a revelation would be there. *Or* ... she was angry anew and about to have revenge relations with the man again. She'd call my apartment and let me hear the sounds, and then tell me she'd made up her mind about getting rid of the baby.

The neighbor's door clicked shut and I rushed down the hall as quietly as I could. I put my ear to the door but heard no voices. A few seconds later, down the hall toward Stan's apartment, another door opened and then quickly shut. But it wasn't Stan. It was 4F across from him. A young man I didn't recognize hurried through the heavy door to the back stairway. I didn't recall anyone coming in or out of that apartment before, but I supposed that wasn't so strange considering I only came here a couple nights a week. I put my ear back to the door. Still no sound. Not a peep.

Do I wait? Do I knock? No more on the defensive!

I turned the knob, found it unlocked, and pushed the door slowly open.

Do I say, "Hello?" Uh, no.

I stepped in and gently shut the door behind me. No one was in the living room or kitchen. A door to the left led to a dark room.

What exactly do I say to the very large man that lives here when he sees me in his apartment?

Nothing, as it turned out.

My eyes slowly adjusted to the dark room where I found the man asleep in a metal-framed twin-sized bunk, his girth stretching the coil springs only a few inches from the floor. One of his big feet sat on the floor, the other jutting several inches off the foot of the bunk. His nose wheezed as he breathed. He didn't have any waves—not even a hint. He had been wiped.

But where was Eileen?

I peered around the room in search of another door, but instead noticed a curtain at the end of the far wall, the shared wall of the next apartment. I walked softly to the curtain and pulled aside a crack. Someone had cut a door-sized opening in the sheetrock, connecting this apartment to the one next door. The room before me was also on the dark side, though not blacked out like the previous one. The windows were all covered in yellowed newspaper. The floors were littered with boxes and stacks of papers. A messy desk occupied one corner, old and/or broken lamps adorned another. The room looked like a reproduction of Gregor's messy legal office.

It wasn't until that last thought flashed through my head that it hit me where I was. I was in Gregor's home. Eileen had walked into *Gregor's* home. The colored man lives in Gregor's home. Was Gregor the colored man? That leering, the smirk, his words—it would make sense. But then I had another thought, something terrible, and I stumbled across the office to the next door. I pulled it open and found another blacked-out room. I stopped moving and tried to hear over my heartbeat in my ear. More breathing. But there were various pitches, out-of-sync breaths. I swept the walls for a switch. I found it and flipped it up. Light shone on six more metal bunks. None of the occupants awoke, of course. Because they weren't asleep.

Two of the beds were empty, but the other four were not. I didn't recognize two of the motionless occupants, a man and an older woman, but the other two—Benny the newsstand guy, and Eileen. Wiped. No waves. I swallowed and tried not to cry. I fought hard to only remember the monster Eileen, not the one that I made love to, or the one that would occasionally say something so shocking that I just had to have a guilty laugh.

I looked at her half-closed eyes and barely-open lips and heard her voice in my head. "You know they all fuck, right?" she had said as we passed a group of priests and nuns. "When church isn't happening, it's nothing but cock swallowing and cum-covered robes." I had been mortified, terrified that someone had heard (someone like God, for instance!), but a quick, cut-off burst of laughter had indeed escaped me. I remembered her looking at me just at that instant, her eyes wide, shocked and thrilled by my reaction, gorgeous smile coming at me, a deep kiss as we walked and almost tripped off the curb. We continued in silence for a short distance, both giggling like little kids in the pews in the middle of the Eucharist after one had passed gas.

She had felt the need to top it all off a moment later. "You know that in Latin 'church' means *fuckhouse*, right?"

"You have to stop," I'd said, now serious. I wasn't comfortable with it going on.

She was mad after that—shut me out for the rest of the walk, called me names under her breath. But standing there, overlooking Eileen's lifeless body, I wanted to think of only the fun part, before it went bad.

I snapped out of it and sighed, walked to the foot of her bunk, and looked her body over. Like the man next door, and the others in the bunks around me, her body was "alive" as far as heartbeat and breathing was concerned, but there was no true life there. But I noticed something and looked closer. Little waves emanated from the side of her belly. The baby.

Suddenly remembering the apartment continued into yet another room, I walked back to the hall and poked my head into the next room. A large messy kitchen area. The kitchen's far wall had yet another curtain. By my estimation, the cutout behind it led to the last apartment, 4F. Gregor had one entire side of the fourth floor. But since when? Had Bryn been more right than I could ever imagine? Was I Gregor's project to *this* extreme?

I walked to the back of the bedroom, between Eileen's bed and the wall where a thick maroon curtain blocked out the midday sun. I reached out a hand on her shoulder and shook.

"Eileen," I whispered near her ear, but of course she didn't respond. She had no more waves of her own. But, again, when did he wipe her? Was that Eileen talking to me at the entrance to the building? It was—in my mind, it absolutely was. Those expressions, that desperate, manipulative manner. So what did it mean? It meant that Gregor had lain in wait upstairs, taking her within minutes of me bidding her farewell.

And what of the colored man in the other room? What of Benny the newsstand guy? These other two? I looked at the faces and suddenly recognized the other woman. Her eyes were open, staring at the ceiling, fingers clasped over her tummy. She was the older lady I had seen outside Gregor's office, going into the office next door. She had given me an odd look, and then shortly thereafter, Gregor was suddenly in his office. She was him. Or he was her.

All these people ... wiped, because of me. Because Gregor wished to play an intricate game.

I looked back at Eileen, curled on her side, one hand draped over her belly. I wondered about the baby. Its waves were faint, but I'd never seen a pregnant woman without waves of her own. It could be how all baby auras appeared from the womb. I wondered if it could still grow and be healthy if its mother was soulless. Something new occurred to me—like a punch in the nose—a thing so unthinkable I felt as though my heart had stopped. It was that final piece, the last clue toward the big solution. I had been on the cusp, but now I no longer wished to solve it. I pushed it away, denied it. I wanted to leave.

Keys rattled outside the 4F door and I heard the squeak of swinging hinges. I ran to the light switch, slapped it off with too loud a strike, and rushed back to Eileen's corner of the room. The door closed and heavy feet with long strides approached. I dropped to the floor beside Eileen's bed, crawled into the corner, and tried to pull my corona all the way in. Would he sense me here? My heart beat so hard in my ears that I covered them, as if it would keep the sound from being audible to others. It only made it louder to me as the muffled footsteps soon entered the room, and stopped.

"Who first, you first," Gregor said in a shrill voice. "Time to get the bellies full."

I saw the springs and thin mattress of one of the empty bunks plummet near the floor as Gregor sat down, then stretched out and lay across it. His gangly frame went still and an instant later, Benny the newsstand guy got up. Benny stretched with a loud groan and walked into the kitchen next door, mumbling.

"Get da belly full, ever felly wool, wet da melly pull, get da belly full ... ."

Pots and dishes rattled and clanked, cupboards opened and closed. With all the noise, I could have run out the way I'd entered, but I was frozen, terrified of what he would do if he found me. Or what he would do to ... Stan.

Stan! The only one left.

If he had wiped Eileen, why wouldn't he do the same to Stan? I had to get him out of there. I had thought he'd be safe if I just left and never came back, but his apartment was only a few feet from Gregor's lair. I had to go, even if I had to borrow Stan's body to get him.

That's it! I ll take Stan out, get him in a cab, use every last bit of money he has to drive as far as possible, then leave him stranded somewhere ... somewhere safe. Perhaps I can write him a note, try to explain.

I made up my mind and dropped out of my body, through the floor to the apartment below. Hoping he didn't sense me leaving, I passed through walls, down the hall, then back up the stairs to the fourth floor. Fearing moving too close to Gregor, I slipped into 4E on my way to Stan's. It looked like a messy department store. Every room was filled with clothing racks, shoe racks, boxes upon boxes with coats and slacks hanging out. Gregor's store room, I deduced. I moved on to Stan's and found what I had feared most. He was crumpled on the floor next to the couch, unconscious. I didn't see any waves coming from him. I tried to nudge him. Nothing. I went inside. Empty. I was too late.

Gregor had finally succeeded in taking away everything I cared about. It was clearly his goal. I didn't play his game the way he wanted, and now I would pay. At that point, the only thing left was the baby in Eileen's womb: surely the most devastating blow a person could imagine. Was that Gregor's plan? Strip me down to nothing? Was there still a plan, or was it simply the chaos?

Whatever it was, I was done losing. It was time that I *took*.

* * *

First, I needed to get my body out of there. I wasn't planning to keep it much longer, thanks to Gregor, but I couldn't let him find out I'd discovered his secret stash of bodies. Not yet, anyway. What I really needed was for Gregor to leave the building and go somewhere far away for a while. Bryn had told me Gregor could sense a daimon taking a new body anywhere in Manhattan, but for me to draw him away, I'd have to actually travel that distance myself, and it wasn't a sure thing.

I continued trying to think of a way to get him out as I made my way back to the fourth floor, entering as far from his kitchen as possible. In 4B, under the bunk of the immobile colored man, I was relieved to hear Gregor still singing "fet da felly bull" as he chopped food.

Perhaps a phone call ... something he couldn't resist going to. A call from the police saying they had me in custody again? That I had specifically asked for him? It could work. I would need to find out the phone number here, though. There were probably multiple lines.

I slowly passed through the last two walls and eased back into my body.

Gregor's song stopped abruptly. "Belly belly swelly swell—" The chopping and stirring sounds ceased as well. He had sensed me. Why didn't I listen to Bryn?

The floor in the kitchen next door creaked ever-so-softly. The sound of wood chair legs sliding a short distance. A boiling pot. The last bunk—the one holding Gregor's "real" body—came to life in an instant. Gregor had sat Benny down on the chair and then moved back to his own body, swinging the legs to the floor and sitting up. Under the beds, I could see the springs depressed beneath his rear end. Then he stood and his feet turned toward me.

"Hmmmm," he hummed. He almost sounded amused. "So sneaky. We have a sneaker in the belfry! A bag in the cat!" I watched his feet step toward the aisle between the two rows of beds. He couldn't see me yet, but he knew I was there. I didn't move. I tried to think but fear had clouded my brain and paralyzed my body. He took another step toward Eileen's bed. One more and he would see my back. As if it mattered. "Oh, what you must think," he said. "So many bodies, eh? Poor Eileen, no? Or is it a relief? Such a disgusting little whore, am I wrong?" He snickered as one of his feet played with the notion of taking another step. "Uh-oh," a theatrical gasp. "You haven't been back to Stan's have you? Oh golly, no. Awfully sad about Stan, especially. Just awful ... strong, genuine friendships can be so difficult to cultivate and sustain."

I shut my eyes and tried to tune out his voice. What could I do? If I got up and ran past him, could he stop me? When he felt my presence here, the first thing he did was return to his body—his preferred body. I presumed to protect it from me.

"Wanna have another go with her? Be in control for once? I assure you she is still *deliciously* juicy. I'll give you some privacy. Just let me know when you're done so I can go shower her off. I have no desire to stir the porridge. *Big* plans for her tonight, too. Even *she* would have blushed at what I'm going to do to her."

I pressed my hands back over my ears.

If I had a gun, I could at least threaten his main body. It might have given me *some* small amount of power over him. But then again, supposedly, he could simply kill me. As in the *real me.* I wondered how much he cared about his other bodies, and then I made a snap decision.

I exited Geoffrey and darted through the walls to the colored man, stood his lumbering body up, and ran for the 4B door. As I ran I heard a fleeting sound from Gregor—a confused chirp. I dashed down the hall and descended the stairway with careless bounds. I was clumsy in the body, never having maneuvered one so large.

"Taxi!" I shouted from the curb, but was passed by several before I gave up and continued fleeing on foot.

A voice from above: "Come on back, buddy!" I glanced up. It was Stan, waving from his fire escape window. "I'll make popcorn!"

I stopped on the other side of the street, my chest heaving. I gazed up at the smirking Stan and decided to go once more with the unpredictable. I sat down on the sidewalk, leaning against the sewing machine shop's brick façade. Stan's head tilted, his face curious. I closed my eyes.

I left the man sitting there and skittered across the street, around to the apartment's rear entrance. I heard nothing in the stairwell and so continued up.

Gregor was smart. He had switched back to his own body to go outside. I was either going to take him or get Geoffrey back, so it worked out either way. And he'd taken the bait.

I jumped back into Geoffrey and opened the curtains, shining surely unwelcome light into the bedroom. I opened the window and took the fire escape down to the alley. There was some small satisfaction in knowing he would be angry when returning to the apartments. Anyone in the adjacent building could now see into his secret room. And I didn't think he would feel as safe about leaving there any time soon. I could come back to take a body at any moment. Judging by his behavior thus far, I didn't think he'd be leaving his own body for a while.

In some small way, I had *won* against Gregor. It didn't come close to making up for Eileen or Stan, or anything else he'd done to me or them, but at that moment, I was grasping for anything positive.

Two blocks north I gazed down the street just in time to see Gregor and someone else carrying the colored man across the street. When they reached the front door of the apartment, the other person came into view. The building manager. Gregor must have gone down and asked for his help with a "drunk friend" or some such excuse.

I hailed a taxi and one stopped right away. I needed to get back to my place and retrieve my money. While Geoffrey Cuion's bank account at First Capital contained a respectable $12,000, I had nearly $300,000 stashed in the box spring beneath my mattress. I would need it for a fresh start somewhere. Well, it wasn't entirely necessary, but it would certainly make it *worlds* easier.

Saturday traffic was light as usual and we made it in less than twenty minutes.

I didn't see any potential police vans on the street (it had occurred to me that calling them would be a perfect play on Gregor's part) and I hurried upstairs. I went straight to my coat closet behind my front door and pulled out an old leather attaché case that would fit all of my cash. On my way to the bedroom I caught a glimpse of something out of place in my peripheral.

I halted and snapped my eyes to the couch and saw two brown shoes extending over the arm. They weren't moving. I took a few hesitant steps forward, craning my neck to see what I knew I wouldn't want to see.

I was right.

It was Bryn, his throat gaping—a pool of blood in the opening, overflowing onto the couch before dripping to the already saturated carpet. I swallowed and touched his cheek. He was still warm. A butcher's knife from my own set rested on the rug beneath his dangling hand.

So I had been partially right about Gregor's next move. The police were surely on their way and there was no way I could cover this up. But I had no intention of staying. I turned to continue to the bedroom.

"Told you we had the right place, Pipes." A sinewy man with greased-back hair, arm tattoos, and leather vest stood in the doorway to my bedroom. A second later, two others appeared behind him. A shorter, wider man with a scruffy beard and red flannel shirt, and "Pipes," who I recognized from outside Gracie's Canteen back in Kansas. He was the one that had tried to stop me from leaving on Tinker's bike.

Pipes—tall, meaty, and blond, with a spiky flat-top—nodded with a little smirk. "Well look at you all fucking smart and fancied up, Tinker. Sorry about your buddy there."

13. Debts

The leader's hand slid from behind his back, revealing a gunmetal revolver. My crestfallen face seemed to satisfy him to no end. His chest swelled and eyelids dipped with evident ecstasy. His bearded friend behind him was not so blissful; he appeared jumpy and afraid of me.

I held my hands out at my sides. "I think there's been some mistake, fellas. Who exactly are you looking for?"

I saw the chubby man's brow contort with confusion. I was certain I sounded nothing like the man he once knew. "Bird, that ain't Tinker, man."

Pipes' smug face changed as he agreed, "Sure don't sound like 'em."

"Bird" stepped forward, unconvinced. He pointed the revolver toward my face and flicked the muzzle to my left. "Look that way."

I turned but kept my eyes on his friends. Their eyes widened at the sight of my scar.

"This is a mistake, gentlemen," I said. "My name is Anthony Sherman. Perhaps if you told me who you were searching for—"

The revolver muzzle smashed into my cheekbone; my eyes clouded with stinging tears. Something hard and blunt struck the top of my skull and I fell to my knees, head ringing.

As if through some distant tunnel, I heard one of Bird's men say, "Why ain't he fightin'?" followed by Bird's very close voice, "'Cause he gone all city faggot! An' 'case you got any other shred'a doubt ... ." My coat was jerked open and back, the buttons of my shirt popped off in a single tearing motion. Bird pulled the shirt over my shoulders and yanked it down to my elbows.

"'Member when I gave you this, Tink?" My right pectoral began to burn. I forced open an eyelid and saw the tip of Bird's Bowie knife twisting into the tattoo on my chest, cutting and pulling. Not deep enough to seriously wound, but the pain quickly grew and I felt dark clouds threatening my brain. "'Bout a month before I gave you *this*, no?" He slit across my jaw scar, reopening half of it. Blood tickled down my neck.

Even before returning home, there remained no more question as to whether or not I'd leave Tinker's body behind, but these animals were seriously complicating the recovery of my mattress money. I knew I could wipe all three of them in just a few seconds, and with little effort, but I was fuming and feeling vindictive. From Gregor to Stan to Eileen, and now Bryn on my couch and this torture, I didn't want to let this scum off easy—I wanted to *hurt*. They would suffer the pain I'd never be able to inflict on Gregor.

"Whoa, whoa, don't fade out on us just yet, Tink!" Pipes said, patting my cheek and handing a length of rope to Bird.

And I *was* fading out. I had been losing consciousness, apparently not immune to it any more than I could resist the need for sleep. Not as long as I was in the body.

"We know you got a stash'a cash," Bird said as he tied up my wrists. "If it's more than the twenty-two grand you owe me, well I'll just be nice an' kill ya. But if it's a penny less, we gonna have us a pain party."

They can help me get the money out. They must have a car, too.

"Mattress ... under," I garbled, but they understood. Pipes disappeared into the other room. The other two followed.

A lamp crashed in my bedroom followed by fabric tearing and gasps.

"Hot damn! Hot damn, look at all that!" Pipes shouted.

"We rich, Bird!" the other one cheered.

But Bird wasn't so sure my $300,000 was an entirely good thing. His face suddenly appeared an inch from mine. His rank breath, like rotting lettuce, invaded my nostrils. "Where you get all this, Tinker? Who you workin' with? Or who you steal it from?"

"All mine ... Nobody else ... ."

He jabbed a grimy finger into the cut in my pectoral. "*Someone's* gonna come lookin' for this goddamn money. Don't you shit me or I'll start cuttin' off parts, small to big."

I repeated, looking in his eyes, "Nobody else."

"You know I know where yer Ma lives. I'll cut that bitch's tiddies off and you know I will."

"It's clear," I said earnestly. "Only mine. Inheritance."

"'Heritance? Hah!" Pipes laughed. "Ain't a Cuion I ever heard'a got more'an a dollar he ain't stole."

Bird whispered in my ear, like an old buddy. Like, *let's set our differences aside and talk turkey.* "Tell the truth now, Tink. Who'd you *herit* from?"

I just stared, done trying to convince these scumbags of anything about *my* money so they could feel good about taking it.

Bird studied me a moment before nodding with a deep breath. "Load it all up and let's get the fuck outta here. J.B., see if you can't find a wallet on dead friend, then drag him in a closet. Give us some extra time to get outta Dodge 'fore someone smells 'em."

J.B. tilted his head to me. "What about Tinker?"

"He's comin' with us," Bird said and turned back to me with a smile. "I know I said I'd let you off quick, but shit, T., when *you* ever stuck to a deal, now? Ain't a time I recall."

"And here I was relying on your honesty and goodwill," I said as I glanced back at Bryn's limp feet hanging off the couch arm.

"Oh don't be sad about yer buddy there," Bird chimed. "He went real quiet-like. We tried to wake him up—Pipes even gave him a solid one to the beak—nothin'. Had a few too many, we reckoned. Din't even wake up when I carved out that throat."

So Gregor had gotten to him first, after all.

Bird went on, "Couldn't have him wake up an' start hollerin' when he seen us tossin' the place. Who's he anyhow? Who's gonna miss 'em?" I shrugged and Bird smiled, wide and toothy. "You got no idea how good it is to see you, Tink. S'like ... like I can be a happy person now, y'know? You been happy all this time?"

Pipes reappeared from my bedroom with suitcase in hand. "Let's roll. How we gonna get him out to the car?"

Bird gazed at me as he scratched his sparse chin hairs. He peered around the room.

"How 'bout we knock 'em out and roll him in this bloody rug? That'll handle a couple'a things."

I didn't like that plan ... Time for me to make my—

A loud thud and then a crash from my coat closet. J.B. popped up from a pile of fallen boxes and coats, and then kicked Bryn's sprawled legs into the closet. I glanced back just in time to see Pipes' large fist flying at my face.

Black.

*   *   *

I awoke with a start, but couldn't gather my bearings for a moment. I was wet, encased, laying prone on my stomach, while gasoline fumes overwhelmed my nostrils. A muffled, erratic tailpipe crooned beneath me. I was rolled up in my Turkish area rug, locked in the trunk of a moving car. The cramped space, lack of air, and my inability to move even an inch sent me plummeting into panic, but then I remembered the obvious...

I left my battered body and entered that of J.B., seated in the backseat. Pipes behind the wheel while Bird counted stacks of money. Where were we? How much time had passed? It was dusk outside. Headlights streamed by in the opposite direction. I ducked J.B.'s head down to catch the passing road sign: HARRISBURG 75mi. We were already in Pennsylvania, driving on Highway 22.

Bird paused counting and scrutinized an upcoming road. "Pull off here."

An unlit dirt road split through a towering grove of red maple trees. Bird reached back with a stack of counted bills. "All hundreds. That's ten grand more. Gimme another stack."

I looked to my right and left, observing neat stacks on one side and Bird's counted stacks on the other. I handed him a fresh stack from my left.

"How far?" Pipes asked.

"Just keep going to a 'spicuous location."

As the car bobbed and jerked down the darkening road, I considered my next moves. Unbeknownst to them, they were taking us to a convenient location for me to ditch their soon-to-be wiped bodies. I would leave two of them with Tinker, take the third (J.B. felt fine) with the car and money, and find some place to lay low for a while before finding a new long-term body. But what about Gregor? Hours of downtime hadn't put much of a damper on my vengeful mood. I have never been a violent individual, but I had been pushed well beyond what I would consider a rational person's threshold. Could I just leave Gregor to his games? Did I have *any* power to affect another outcome?

Pipes turned down an even thinner side road, outstretched branches scratching along the windows and doors.

Bird looked up from the cash in his lap. "Don't get us trapped now, idiot."

"I ain't, it's fine, look." He pointed down the road where the curtains of trees widened out into a circular dead end. The headlights wiped across pale tree trunks as he brought the car around and stopped. "Whaddya think?"

"Let's have a listen," Bird said as he handed the cash back to me and opened his door. "Privacy is a virtue, they always say."

I don't think they ever say that.

I thought it a good time to return to my body. J.B. would think he'd simply nodded off.

The crisp sound of buzzing insects through J.B.'s ears turned to the muffled bass of the idling car through the rug. Squeaky doors opened and closed. My body was dizzy—probably low on oxygen and high on gasoline. Fumes aside, it was difficult to inhale more than short breaths while compressed so tightly. If they didn't get me out soon, I'd have to make new plans.

The engine was shut off and the trunk opened. I was hefted out by both ends and then dropped a few feet to the ground. Increasingly painful kicks unrolled the rug until I found myself splayed on the ground; cool, fresh air suddenly filling my lungs. The scents of rich soil and spicy sassafras. Headlights between standing legs blinded me.

Pipes' voice: "I say we soften 'em up a while, cut some shit off, then burn 'em."

J.B. snickered. "Maybe we just skip to the burnin'!"

"Nah I def'ley gotta sweat 'em," Bird said as he pulled his large Bowie knife from its sheath on his hip. "That's a debt longer waitin' than my money. Din't think you'd ever have to pay that one back, eh Tink? Long forgot?"

"You gonna sweat 'em, Bird?" J.B. sounded nervous and excited.

What exactly is this "sweating" business?

Wrists still tied behind me, I labored up onto my knees.

"Ain't you gonna say nothin', Tink?" Pipes sounded disappointed. "Almost makin' me feel bad. An' that fuckin' mouth'a yours always did inspire some rage in me. C'mon, be a sport."

I looked up at their silhouettes and smiled. "All three of you are going to die."

Bird and Pipes burst into laughter. J.B. forced a small cackle, but I could hear a little fear in him.

"That's not too bad!" Pipes laughed. "Keep on!"

"Go get the gas," Bird said through chuckles. J.B. complied as Bird turned to Pipes. "Cut his wrists free and hold onto 'em."

I saw Pipes hesitate for an instant, almost uttering a protest. *Can't we keep him tied up?* I imagined him wanting to say. Tinker's apparent formidable reputation persisted, even in my slacks and torn Oxford. In two long strides, Pipes was on me, towering. A stinging punch to my ear, then an even stronger blow to the base of my neck, where it meets the shoulder. I crumpled to the ground and pleaded with myself to wait ... just wait.

A switchblade snapped behind me and I felt my bindings loosen then fall away. Just as I began to sit up and bring my hands forward to stretch out and massage my wrists, Pipes pulled them back by the elbows, tearing shoulder muscles as he lifted me to my feet. Darkness briefly clouded over me and I suddenly became aware that I could be knocked out again at any time, and this scum could drive off with my money, never to be seen. I needed to act fast.

I opened my eyes, startled to find Bird only a few inches from my face.

"Now it's time I sweat you like you sweat me, fucker!"

It happened so fast I didn't grasp what he'd done until Pipes raised my hands up over my head. Bird had cut me open at the armpits. One vertical slice each. Skin tore further as Pipes held my arms up and blood oozed down my sides. I only realized I was screaming after J.B. hurled gasoline at me and I choked and spat it up. My eyes burned as if already on fire.

"Fucker!" Pipes shouted. "You got it all over me!"

But J.B. kept pouring the gas, spraying it all over me and Pipes.

Pipes had let go and I fell back to the dirt, unmoving. Well, *Tinker's* body fell. *I* had moved into J.B. after the first splash of gas and had continued pouring, ensuring Pipes got nice and saturated. Pipes shoved me (J.B.) back by the throat. The gas can fell and tumbled, the remaining liquid glugging out into the soil.

"The fuck's wrong with you?" Pipes shouted. "Fucking *idiot!* Don't light anything! Don't nobody light anything!" He stomped off toward the car.

I glanced at Bird, who was giving me the slow no-nod. He spoke like a disappointed father. "That was real fuckin' stupid, John. He gonna fuck you up later."

I looked down at my unmoving Geoffrey body, then back at Pipes undressing by the car. He tossed his vest into the back seat, balled up his T-shirt and threw it in the dirt at his feet, then examined his jeans.

"Down my fucking pants, too, asshole!"

"He gonna fuck you up good. You might wanna offer him up some'a yer share or somethin'. Somethin' to ease 'em back, you know?"

I nodded and reached into J.B.'s front pockets, finding what I hoped would be there. Right beneath a soft pack of cigarettes: the smooth outline of a Zippo lighter.

"Howsa'bout I just set him on fire?" I said and flicked the lighter open. Bird's expression seemed to say *well **no**, that probably wouldn't be too smart* ... as flintwheel scraped flint, and flame rose from the lighter. Bird's face morphed to confusion and then horror as I tossed the lighter through the air, his eyes tracing the arc to Pipes' gas-soaked T-shirt at his feet by the car. Pipes sat on the edge of the back passenger seat, struggling to remove a boot.

The flames engulfed him in less than a second just as I realized what I'd done. The saturated leather vest in the backseat went up too, quickly followed by my stacks of cash.

"What did you do?" Bird screamed and lurched at me as Pipes howled and flailed and bounced around in the back of the car.

We rolled in the dirt for a moment, Bird not even close to understanding what was going on. Even when I yanked the revolver from his belt and pointed it at his stomach, he still said "What now? No! Quit that, you idiot! We gotta put 'em out—" Even after I fired a shot into his gut, it only worsened his confusion. He looked at the blood dribbling over his fingers, gawked at J.B.'s face, looked down at the blood flowering across his shirt. "John ... ."

I pushed him off me and shot him in the middle of his bewildered face.

Pipes had stopped moving in the backseat, but the flames had overtaken the whole interior of the car.

Now what?

My escape vehicle and decades of accumulated wealth were gone in a flash. I had had big plans for that money.

But I felt *good* about Bird's dead body beside me. I felt *good* about the two feet dangling out the backseat of the car, one covered with a charred, flaming boot, the other bare and burning.

Nearby, the body of Geoffrey Cuion lay in a heap on its side. I wondered if it was dead yet, and then I remembered something else. My bank account! It wasn't anything close to my mattress money, but if my body was still alive I could walk into my bank's lower Manhattan branch, and walk out with $12,000 of new start money. That much could cover a new car, and first and last on an apartment, with plenty left over until I had stable work somewhere. That is, *if* my body was still alive. If not, what could I do? Write a check to J.B.? Would that work for the entire balance in the account?

I stuffed the revolver into the back of J.B.'s pants, crouched down beside my body, and checked to see if I was still breathing. Tinker was indeed a tough S.O.B. Still alive for now. But I had to get him to a hospital before he bled out through his armpits. Plus, he was covered in gasoline a short distance from a raging fire. I started to drag him away by the arms but quickly halted, wincing at the sight of the "sweating" wounds.

"Sorry," I said and put his arms across his chest, switching to his ankles to drag him.

I pulled him a good fifty yards from the fire before leaving him to go find a car or telephone.

* * *

I found a farmhouse several miles down the main dirt road. I walked the majority of the way since J.B. didn't seem to have the healthiest lungs or a scrap of stamina when I tried to run. There were only two lights on, the porch and another on the second floor. I was relieved to find the keys to their new Ford pickup dangling from the ignition.

Dogs began barking when I started the engine and another light turned on upstairs. I peeled out backward, rolled the wheel around, and took off up the road before I saw anyone come out. My body was still alive when I pulled it into the cab, and still alive when I carried it past a clutch of horrified nurses smoking outside the emergency room in Allentown.

"This man is dying!" I shouted, and my former body was quickly eased onto a rolling stretcher as a doctor fired questions at me.

I explained, "He's a friend of mine ... gang of drunk men attacked him outside a bar ... ."

I witnessed more than a couple frowns at Tinker's tattoos as he was examined.

"He's a Navy war hero!" I proclaimed. "Served in Korea!" That seemed to inspire them. He was enveloped in white uniforms and wheeled off.

I slipped out before anyone could ask further questions, confident that if anything could be done to save my body—and my access to my bank account—these people would do it.

I drove the pickup for a couple blocks and pulled over.

What to do?

I would have to wait for my Geoffrey body to heal before attempting a bank run. In the meantime, I'd need to hide out ... or do something. The image of Gregor as Stan smiling down at me from his apartment window. Pregnant Eileen curled on her side in the bunk. Gregor's shrill, leering voice, "Big plans for her tonight, too. Even *she* would have blushed."

I asked myself what I actually *wanted*. What did I wish to accomplish before moving on to a new life? I tried to determine what would not just feel good, but what would be *right?* I had some ideas, both ludicrous and reasonable. The unrealistic plans felt the best, but they wouldn't do me any good. I needed to be logical, methodical, and to think how Gregor would think.

The elements of a plan began taking shape in my mind.

14. Honor Among Thieves

Before returning to New York I had to practice something with J.B. I needed to know if I could leave an instruction or memory of a task in his head the way Gregor had with Stan, sending him to the fire escape, thinking he needed to "check on something."

My initial implant was simple: *You need to walk casually for three blocks.*

Inside his head, I moved close to the little J.B. huddled in a dark corner of his mind, thinking he was having a dream. I whispered the instruction to him, repeated it, and left his body to see the results. J.B. came to, looked around with panic, and began running away in a zigzagging pattern, glancing back as if being chased. I wondered if he knew I was in there—heard me in his head not as some other part of his own psyche, but as an actual invasive entity, a voice from the outside. I caught up to him, hopped back in, and tried again.

My second attempt was equally ineffective. J.B. looked at our stolen truck on the side of the road, peered down the sidewalk where I'd told him to go, then he shook out his head and began walking to the truck.

A short while later I figured out *what* I needed to do, but it wasn't until a full half hour after that that I finally grasped *how* to do it. J.B. had to be in control when I gave him the instruction. Unfortunately, I had never taken the backseat when in a body. I didn't even know the process. It took numerous tries just to get this first part down, and in the end I couldn't determine the procedure one utilizes to go from front seat to back seat. I had to start from the outside, with J.B. completely in control of himself, and then jump in, straight to the backseat. I was certain that Gregor had all this down, and that one day, if I survived the next twenty-four hours, I'd be able to perfect it, but in the meantime I had a thoroughly terrified J.B. literally banging his head against the hood of the truck. He believed himself insane or, yes, possessed by a demon. Absent some memory-erasing maneuver, I had essentially ruined him for the job. But I still needed him. He would just play a different role in the plan.

I went back into him in the traditional manner, shoving his consciousness to the background, and drove toward the city. For my plan to work, Gregor had to be home in his apartment, and my earlier notion that he would choose to stick in or around the building seemed to remain the likeliest situation. If he wasn't home, however, I guessed my job would be easier than I expected, albeit much less predictable. Most critical, after setting things in motion, I had to know that Gregor would be gone a while.

* * *

I parked the truck about a mile from Gregor's building and walked the final stretch with my corona pulled in as best as I could maintain. I kept my eyes peeled, scanning both sides of the street. There were pedestrians about, some in couples, some alone. I needed an unaccompanied person, and the right sort. Someone at whom Gregor wouldn't look twice.

An elderly woman with a bag of groceries appeared promising, but I wouldn't be able to move her fast enough. A woman was good, though. Gregor didn't seem to care about genders—I presumed that after thousands of years, his personal gender identity had blurred—but he knew that I had only ever used male bodies. He might not expect a female.

Three blocks from the building, I spotted her. She was walking quickly, her curly black locks protruding from a headscarf, creating a hair cowl in which she could hide from the world. Her arms were crossed before her as she walked, a tiny purse on a short chain clutched at her belly. I waited for a car to pass, then walked across the street to intercept her. As we neared each other, her eyes darted from me to the ground and back, her path changing to evade me, but I shifted course right along with her until we both stopped, face to face. She wore thick glasses that enlarged her eyes to a comical size and her huge upper teeth perched over her lower lip like talons on a branch. Though she had adorned herself like an older woman, I guessed she was in her mid-twenties.

"What?" she exclaimed in a bird-like falsetto, hands balled and ready to strike. Her voice was oddly deep. "What?" she repeated, louder.

I pulled the revolver from the back of my pants—J.B.'s pants—and pointed it at her. She gawked at it, and for a moment I thought she might just keel over and die, right there in front of me.

"What's your name?" I demanded.

"Prudrent ... Strudence ... ." she spluttered and then squeezed her eyes to concentrate and get it out. "Prudence!"

"Good." I scratched my beard and glanced around to be sure no one was paying us any mind. "Prudence, I need you to take this gun from me, or I feel I might rob somebody. Can you help me?"

Her eyes remained warped saucers behind the lenses.

"Quickly now, Prudence!" I exclaimed in a hush. "I don't want to hurt anybody!"

Shaking hands sprouted from her belly, fingers slowly curling around the pistol, and she pulled it back to her, not wanting to look at it.

I shared a kind smile. "Thank you. Now don't drop that."

Next, I crept back to J.B., hunched and rocking in the back of his head. I went right to his little soul-face and blared in the most frightening voice I could muster.

"You make a deal with the devil, the devil takes his payment! I've got you now, John! Get ready for my hell hounds to feast on your innards! Here they come!"

And then I leapt straight from J.B. to Prudence. J.B. came to life like his feet were on fire, but he didn't know which way to go.

"They're coming!" I screamed with Prudence's voice and pointed behind me in the direction of Gregor's building. "Get a taxi! You can't outrun them on foot!"

J.B. nodded wildly, searched the street for cabs, and flailed his arms high. I watched several pass him before he finally ran in front of one. The driver squealed to a stop, cursed, but J.B. got in and away he went. I turned around and walked toward Gregor's apartment, doing my best to imitate Prudence's harried shuffle, my corona locked in tight. I hoped that I had understood Bryn correctly about bodies leaving trails. He had said that when transferring bodies, the act itself can be sensed within a certain geographical area, and that the person you exited leaves a trail. I would soon see if I had properly grasped the concepts.

With one block to go and the building in sight on the other side of the street, I was gratified and relieved to see Gregor's lank form strolling this way. He wore a beige suit with a matching trilby hat, tipping the brim to each passer-by. We passed on opposite sides of the street and I did not look back until I'd made it to the next intersection. I glanced down the block to see Gregor bowing deep to enter a taxi. When it was out of sight, following the same course I'd seen J.B.'s taxi drive, I ran to the apartment building and in the front door.

I hid the revolver behind the stairs and left Prudence in the small lobby, figuring there would be no need to help her out with any instructions to make her leave. Indeed, as I ascended the stairs, she poked her head out the glass doors, scanned both directions with confusion, and dashed out, resuming her stroll.

On the fourth floor, the dark bedroom looked just as it had the first time I saw it, but upon switching on the light, I discovered a new addition. Stan lay in the first bunk, his eyelids open a crack. My mission would be more difficult than I'd thought. Occupying Stan or Eileen would not be easy for me, emotionally, but my time was limited and I needed to move. I looked at their faces. Who first?

The little waves slow dancing around Eileen's belly helped me to decide. I went inside her, stood her up, and touched her face, her perfect skin. And then I felt her belly.

Go!

I ran out through 4F, down the back stairs, and out to the alley where I realized she was barefoot. The cool concrete felt good on her feet, but I worried about stepping on glass or other hazards. What if I fell with the baby? What if I'd fallen down the stairs? Was it even safe to run with a baby inside? I walked at a fast pace, two blocks west and four blocks south to the new Frances Martin Library. At the service entrance I reached under and behind the utility meter box, through unseen cobwebs, and found the spare key where I hoped it still hid.

Inside, I walked Eileen to the warehouse store room, laid her down under the shipping desk, and left her body.

I raced back to the apartment in a straight line, passing through walls, garages, rooms with glowing families watching TV, a tree trunk, a mailbox.

I took Stan next, sadness pulsing through me as I ran my friend's empty body to the library, laying him down in front of Eileen. I continued with each of them, ending with Benny the newsstand guy, standing in Gregor's otherwise empty apartments, the rest of his stolen bodies hidden safely (I hoped) inside the library warehouse. I shut off the light, noted the number on one of Gregor's telephones, then took Benny to the library.

Next, I needed to get away from them, borrow a new body—one Gregor wouldn't recognize. I checked the watch on

Benny's wrist. 9:45 p.m. I laid him down with the rest and hopped out.

Outside, I found a number of people standing at a bus stop. A tall, younger man stood away from the main group, staring at the rear end of a young colored lady in front of him. It wasn't much to justify taking him, but I wasn't going to wipe him, just use him for the night. I jumped in and strolled up the street just as the bus approached and people streamed out the exits. This new body belonged to Pascal Pratt, whom I found drenched in sweat despite the chilly night air. I quickly discovered that, as it seems is too often my luck, the man had to defecate—and with some urgency. I cursed in my head and hurried back toward Gregor's building.

At the alley entrance I peered up at all of his windows, observing no shadows or signs of movement. Up the back stairs, into the fourth floor laundry room, I grabbed Stan's spare key and let myself into his apartment.

I left the lights off, rushed to the bathroom, and handled Pascal's business for him. Just as I was cleaning up, I heard the distinctive footsteps of a very tall individual in the floor's main hall behind me. Keys rattled, a door opened and shut.

I fastened my pants and eased back to the living room, pressing my ear to the wall. I counted down in my head. *3 ... 2 ... 1 ...*

A massive crash, piercing shrieks.

I smiled.

Gregor was so loud I didn't have to listen at the wall. I was certain everyone in the building could hear him. Soon, he would come thrashing out the door in search of his stolen bodies, but I needed to speak with him first. I tiptoed to Stan's phone and dialed Gregor's phone number. A few seconds later, I heard the muffled ring, followed by a series of stomps.

The call picked up and I spoke before he could. "Lose something?"

His screaming response came through as loud static. Beyond the walls I could distinguish "assfuck" and "erase" and "die" among the cacophony. When he was done I heard only wheezing breaths, as if the receiver was inside his mouth.

"That sounds like a really big tantrum, Gre—"

He began again, crashes and shattered glass in harmony with his unintelligible shrieks.

"Gregor?" I attempted. "Gregor?" Until he finally calmed down and the panting in the phone resumed. "Listen to me, Gregor. I'm going to be watching you ... ."

"Watching!?" He squeaked.

"... and anyone you take, I'm going to take them from you." A lie. I had no intention of staying anywhere near the state, let alone the city.

"You?! You take nothing! *You* are nothing! You have no idea, motherfucking blighter drehzeel agah'tach ... ." he went on in some language I couldn't identify.

"Yes, me," I said calmly once he'd paused. "Bryn taught me a lot before you got to him, more than—"

"I taught you nothing!" he shouted. "I taught you *shit!* Bryn ... you imbecile ... there was never a Bryn!"

Never a Bryn?

His voice went low and close in my ear. "I will keep you in a body, slide out the fingernails, tweeze apart eyes, *rip* the flesh in strips if you don't bring ... her ... back! You will suffer as no one in this age has suffered! I will reinvent *pain* before I kill you!"

"You were Bryn ... ." was all I could say.

"How stupid are you, boy? Are you such an infant? There was never a Bryn, never an Eileen, never a Stan ... You never met any of them! You never knew those people! What they left behind, that's mine, not yours! Now keep the rest if you wish, but you bring her back *now!"*

Never a Stan ... Gregor was Stan?

I had begun to get it. Gregor was Bryn, playing me, keeping me a part of his game, encouraging me to stick with Gregor, make a deal. He was Benny at the newsstand ... of course! All the people supposedly helping me. But Stan? For how long? He said "never a Stan," which meant ... *Oh God ... from the very beginning.* Mark's on Park.

How to catch a daimon's attention? Tell them a story about another daimon. The truth was settling in, and I would have to reconcile my friendship with Stan later, but my shattered mind wasn't ready to accept one part.

"But who was Eileen then, if not her?"

Gregor adopted Eileen's tone and inflections. "Jesus fucking Christ, Geoffrey! Must I color you a goddamn picture? I always knew you weren't a man, but a fucking idiot?"

Pascal's stomach seized and turned with nausea. Bile erupted into my mouth.

"The whole time?" I thought out loud. "Why? For what purpose? All for the game?"

Gregor's voice returned. "The *game?* Stop listening to Bryn. There is no game! Bryn hasn't existed for three hundred years. But silver-haired Jim? That sack was a fucking accountant. If you don't understand what was going on, then don't bother thinking about it because you never will."

For an instant it sounded as if Gregor's feelings were hurt. But that quickly disappeared.

"Now listen to me close, little boy. That young woman is *mine.* She was *given* to me. *Most* of my bodies were *given* to me, not *stolen* as you have stolen from me. The real her—*Nora*—went off in a new body to Spain or Greece or some such destination. I found her, made a deal, gave her immortality, and now her shell belongs to *me.* Mine. You have no right … ."

Never an Eileen. Gregor was Eileen.

Descartes's *Meditations* popped up in my mind. *Strip away belief in all things that are not absolutely certain, and then try to establish only that which can be known for sure.* And as he always did, with Descartes came Quincy. Quincy was back in my mind, along with all the horrible shit memories that surrounded him. *The bad time.* Now piled on top of a new *bad time,* intermingling, perhaps with more similarities than I wished to acknowledge. I wanted to crumple and give up. What was I fighting for? How much of my life could I say was truly good? How many years of my life weren't even *real?* Why was this happening to me? Quincy—once the cause of a similar quandary—would no doubt have brilliant, eye-opening observations on the matter, but I didn't want to think about Quincy. I didn't want to think about Eileen, Stan, Gregor.

If all Gregor had said was true, what was my purpose now? Why persist with my plan? Revenge? Punishment? As I sat on the phone, stewing, I decided I was okay with those rationales.

He was still ranting. "… any shred of honor, of what's right … everyone knows there are just some things you don't do."

I finally interrupted him. "You're going to try to appeal to my sense of fair play? Honestly? After what you've done! There is a baby in—"

"The child isn't yours, Geoffrey! The child is mine. It's *me* … to *be* me … It's mine, and it's none of your concern. Give her back and I'll let you live. Bring. Her. Back."

Revolted and stunned I said, "What are you going to do, give birth to yourself?"

"It's none of your concern!" he said and then screamed, *"It's none of yours!"*

The final piece of the puzzle laid, it was all solved. Everything finally made sense, for as sickening the revelations were, I got them. The baby *was* Gregor's. He had impregnated a lifeless Eileen.

"That baby has a soul, I've seen it. You're going to wipe your own child and use it for your next body?" As the words left my lips, I suddenly realized why he was so attached to his grotesque body. It was his real body, in some sense—the body of some descendent, a centuries-long lineage—his only connection to his original self. Surely some inbreeding along the way … perhaps his selection of Eileen, or "Nora" as he said she was called, was to try to inject some of that beauty into his line. Offset his deformities and asymmetry with what she—no, *he*—had always tried to tout with me. Her perfection. She'd messed up the word symmetry, but of course I could not correct her ... *him*. It made me ill once more to think back to a conversation and rewrite it with Gregor as Eileen.

He'd said, "Did you know that beauty is when things are balanced? It's called symmetrics. I have perfect symmetrics."

I decided right there that I would give him his next body back, the baby, but it would be my way, and I'd be taking something in exchange.

I went on, "If that child is really yours—"

Gregor turned shrill and scary again. "Don't you even *try* to make a deal with me, cocksucker! You're bringing her back or I'm erasing everyone you ever cared about!"

"An interesting threat," I quipped.

"Right. Well, how's this for a threat? I could wipe every single person on this island. One or two seconds each, thirty a minute, on to the next, eighteen hundred an hour, forty-three thousand in a day—you know I don't sleep—how many souls in the city? You know I will to get what I want. And, oh, if you don't ... I *know* what it is *you* want, Samuel. I know what you've been missing. At some point you'll stop being a boring, whining little sissy faggot and find yourself a nice hunk of woman flesh, someone that not only fucks you like you want, but that *loves* you the way you want to be loved. She'll squeeze out a couple of rugrats for you and you'll *love* them, too, like nobody's ever loved! And then who's going to show up? Take a guess! You have a mildly creative mind ... What do you think is the *worst* thing I could do in that situation? I don't know what's worse, the kids first or the wife first, but we'll have to wait and see. Oh fuck ... yes ... what if one of the kids kills the other kid *and* their mom? Maybe the other way around—we'll have to see. And I won't kill *you*, no way. You'll have to figure a way out of that hell on your own."

The soft hum of an open telephone line. His breath was slow, waiting. I thought about what he'd said—all of it, not just the threats. He waited.

I finally spoke. "I'm going to give her back to you."

"Yes," he said, as if confirming I'd provided the right answer to a quiz question.

"But I'm not bringing her there."

"No?"

"I don't feel safe there. I don't know what you're going to do to me once you have her."

"A valid concern for a fucking thief. Go on."

"So I'm going to bring her to a park, later tonight when no one's around. Let's say two a.m., Gorman Park in Washington Heights."

"A long time to leave me waiting, Samuel."

A bit of Eileen had slipped back into his voice—playful, as if we were planning some sex game.

"And you come in your *real* body," I added. "Not some loaner you don't care about."

"Mmm ... so logical. I hate to say it, but I like this manly side of you, Geoffrey. When things are all settled here, you wanna make it up to me and fuck me proper? In her body, of course."

"You disgust me," I spat, and I'm certain he knew I was speaking to Eileen, not Gregor. "Always have. Maybe I'll just shoot her and save some other poor guy from this sort of torture."

"Don't you fucking think it—"

"We'll see, Gregor! I have some deliberating to do."

I slammed the phone down, and regretted it instantly. The ringer bell chimed and echoed in Stan's apartment. I clutched the phone to my chest to silence it, but it was too late. I heard Gregor's stomps approaching, a door crashed, Stan's door exploded open, and there he was, large butcher knife in hand. I leapt back, out of the body, just as Gregor's knife plunged into Pascal Pratt's stomach.

Sorry, Pascal ... It wasn't supposed to end that way.

I floated through the window and dropped four stories to the street, through the surface, and stopped myself in a large sewer pipe. I followed it north for several miles before emerging back at street level.

Now I just had to wait, and I hoped that Gregor decided to be prompt. I wasn't going to go hopping into Eileen's body while Gregor was still a few blocks away. I'd wait until he was all the way in Washington Heights, then go get her. Make him sweat for a half an hour waiting for me.

God, I hated him, but he would soon pay for everything he'd done.

* * *

I had decided not to acquire any shoes for Eileen. It would work better that way. The one thing I did need, though, was the pistol I had Prudence hide beneath the stairs. I returned to the apartment building, reached under the stairs, and picked up the revolver. I folded the gun into the extra material in her dress and waited a few minutes for a cab to appear. Eileen never had any problems hailing cabs.

The crew-cut cabby threw an arm over his passenger seat and eyed me. "Why you don't got no shoes, pretty lady?"

"Raging foot fungus," I said. "They must have air at all times."

The cabby nodded, faced forward, and remained silent the rest of the drive.

I cannot describe how surreal it felt to be in Eileen's body, to use her voice. It was her voice, but not entirely. As I had learned from the male bodies I'd used, the voice box is one thing, but how a person uses it is another. It takes practice to match a prior occupant. I realized then that the Eileen voice I knew was a combination of this body's sound and the intonation Gregor had used on the phone.

I looked down at her cleavage, her legs. I tried not to think about the fact that this flesh I was occupying had never been a real woman—at least as long as I'd known it. I tried not to think about how the body had been *used*, over and over, like some toy. Nor did I wish to think about the men other than me that had used it. Though I wasn't planning to use Geoffrey's body much longer, I felt that my very soul—*my real being*—had been dirtied by Gregor and this female body. Defiled and debased forever.

I had the driver drop me off a block from the meeting spot. I padded up the sidewalk, observing the lightless windows of the surrounding buildings. Beat-up, overflowing garbage cans lined the street between parked cars. A powdery gray cat groomed its groin atop the presumably warm hood of a car. The area was as close to silent as a New York City neighborhood could get.

I passed the last building before Gorman Park's small footprint opened up a patch of starry sky. The park had more trees than I'd remembered, its sloped terrain more sloped. The apartments on the opposite side appeared as sleepy as its neighbors.

Not for long, I hoped.

I held the revolver in one hand, and with the other kept Eileen's dress up at her knees. I walked onto the moist grass, the wet soil beneath oozing up between her toes with each step. As I'd hoped, not a soul was about, in the park or on the bordering streets. I moved behind a tree and peeked around the trunk to the central clearing. No Gregor.

I remained in the dark shadows, creeping from tree to tree to check out the other side of the park, but I didn't see him anywhere. Perhaps I'd made him wait too long. Or maybe he was on to me, knew not to trust me—

"Leave her," Gregor's voice close behind me. I spun around. He loomed high overhead, his little black pig eyes shining from the street lights below. Brown suit minus the jacket, his pale yellow shirt was tucked and sharp, sleeves rolled to his elbows. "You make me wait this long, it gets me thinking maybe I *do* want to kill you after all. Now get out!"

I backed around the tree, keeping my eye on him, and pointed the revolver at Eileen's belly. "Don't come any closer."

Gregor saw the gun and released a strange chirp. "Drop that thing! How dare you! An unborn child?"

"Yes, and I'll kill it without a second thought if you try anything. If you leave your body, I will squeeze this trigger. So stay right there."

I continued moving backward in the grass as Gregor sidestepped to keep me in view, glaring at me and murmuring. I continued back until we had a good bus length between us, away from the cover of trees. Gregor stood seething but shrewdly passive. I peered around at all the balconies and windows in the adjacent apartment buildings.

"Now what?" he called. "You came to give her back to me, so now what, Geoffrey? Are you going to make me tell you some bullshit promise I may or may not keep?" He shook his head and took a step toward me. "You're not going to shoot a baby."

I cocked the revolver, as they always did in the movies. "You positive about that?"

He put up his hands and smirked. "Fine, fine, little boy. Let's hurry it up then. What do you want?"

"Nothing much," I said and pointed the gun at him. I squeezed the trigger, again and again, unloading the remaining four rounds into his chest. I saw the look of fear, confusion, the striving to understand. On his knees, his treasured body dying, Gregor's eyes suddenly locked on mine. He'd gotten it.

I smiled, sat Eileen down on her knees, and waited.

"You'll never ... ." he choked and tried to suck in air. It didn't look like his lungs were working too well for him. He mouthed words, clearly angry ones, but the fear was still there, until finally, it wasn't. His expression turned to nothing and his body collapsed into a pile. I flew out the back of Eileen just as Gregor arrived there. He was faster than I had anticipated; I was lucky I got out in time. I watched him stand her up, curl her hands around her belly, shoot daggers in every direction.

"Never over, Geoffrey!" she screamed. "Never ... fucking ... over!"

That may be true, I thought, *but you're cut off from your business, wealth, possibly your home, and are soon going to be an infant for at least a little while.*

I watched as windows lit up throughout the neighborhood. Tentative onlookers peeped through curtains, some even venturing out onto their balconies. Gregor stood there, out in the opening where I had moved Eileen's body.

Police sirens echoed between the buildings and I saw Gregor look in horror at the gun in his hand.

And hopefully in a prison.

It may have been shortsighted of me, but I just couldn't leave him in the perfect world he'd set up around him. It may not have been as devastating as what he'd done to me, but when the first police car screeched to a stop against the park curb and the two officers stepped out with guns drawn, I felt that I hadn't done too badly for myself after all.

I left as the second and third patrol cars rolled to a stop at the other side of the park, and one of Eileen's hands went up in the air as the other pointed frantically at her pregnant belly. That was the image I wished to keep with me. Gregor may have "gotten me" hundreds of times and left many permanent scars, but at least I had this. Just this once, I had gotten *him*.

15. Epilogue - New Lives

The Pennsylvania doctors did a good job patching up Geoffrey, but couldn't ascertain which element of his trauma had caused the coma. Admittedly due to cowardice (I have an aversion to pain), I remained an invisible observer in his room for several days. The amount of physical suffering I'd recently endured was not something I wished to continue or ever experience again. Likewise on the emotional agony, but I hoped I had at least *reduced* the risk of another Gregor encounter by several factors.

Doctors congratulated themselves upon Geoffrey's awakening, told me I'd given them quite a scare, and upon release, I made my way to my bank's nearest branch to close my account. The teller couldn't hide her shock at my appearance: brown-and-blue face, bandaged jawline where Bird sliced open my scar, my arms wrapped tight to my sides at the elbows to keep me from ripping open the stitches in my armpits.

"Horrific accident," I said. "They say I'm lucky to be alive."

I slid the slip on the counter a little closer to her. She finally broke her gaze and got the manager to approve my withdrawal. Stack of cash in a small bank pouch, I walked out and breathed a sigh of finality. I was free.

Or was I?

You don't experience what I went through without carrying a constant twinge of dread in the back of your mind. Something bad is going to happen, because it always does. You can shove this feeling to the background, even go through days without knowing it's there, but it's there. Standing in the bank parking lot, my eyes darted from a man exiting his car to a passing woman who glanced at me with what I perceived to be recognition. A young man walked his dog across the driveway. Someone sat smoking on a balcony above.

I found a payphone and called the precinct, asking for Detective Morton. He was surprised to hear from me. He'd already heard that Eileen was arrested and gone to see her at the jail where she was being held. She was apparently trying to seduce every cop that came by.

"Got caught blowing one of her guards through the bars last night," he said with unveiled amusement. "Still a lot of questions we need answered and this broad ain't doin' it for us." He wanted me to come in to talk about why she might have killed my lawyer. "Where are you right now? I'll send a car out to give you a ride to the station. A *front* seat ride, if you're worried."

"I don't think so, Detective," I said. "As much as I've enjoyed our talks in the past."

I hung up.

At least I knew Gregor was still in custody as I made my way out of town.

My escape plan was simple: travel far, commit to a body, live a long, healthy life, and only transition when absolutely necessary. If at all possible, switch bodies in a remote area. Given that Bryn had always been Gregor, I had to take his words with a grain of salt. Was Gregor's ability to sense a daimon's entry truly geographically limited?

I traveled south with Tinker, found a secluded area, and spoke a few words beginning with "If you're out there and can hear me ... ." Not so much an apology as much as hoping he was in a better place, wishing him well, et cetera. Who knows, perhaps if I hadn't taken him that day in the bar restroom, Bird would have killed him right then! I know, it's justification and rationalization, but it's what I do. I do not pretend my morals are beyond reproach, but I do the best I can, considering.

After leaving Tinker, I hunted for certain signs in a nearby suburb, eventually discovering Clyde, a man with no criminal record but with a deplorable and dangerous craving for pubescent girls. Fortunately, I got to him before he'd been caught doing anything, so he was free of Tinker's sort of legal burdens, and after "wiping" him, I could enjoy the same lack of associated guilt. I moved Clyde out of his native town to a new state, got an apartment, an unfulfilling job as a custodian, and kept to myself. I read a *lot.*

Looking back, I could call that period my reading years, because it seems I did little else. Being alone, despite everything I had always thought essential for true happiness, I had finally found peace. I may have only been in the equivalent of forties or fifties, mental age-wise, but it was sort of like retirement. Retirement from the world of interpersonal relationships.

Still, it wasn't all roses being alone. I mean, honestly ... I was *alone.* There was depression, emptiness. I didn't have dark days—I had dark months. However, through the ups and downs, there was always something comforting in the background, knowing that I could end that period whenever I was ready.

The time came when Clyde's body decided it was tired of me: lung cancer.

There were a few things I had unwaveringly avoided in those two decades that I resolved to seek in my next life. I wanted to grow up in a loving family, form those bonds, and then build a family of my own. I felt blessed to have the longevity and *condition* to go on living, to have the continuing opportunity to build the life of my dreams.

I fully appreciate what I have now, and know that for most everyone else there are no second chances. Indeed, I eventually found the family I always wanted. After generations of failure and tragedy when it came to relationships—seemingly without exception—I took a chance and struck gold. I found the girl of my dreams and married her. I have children that I love more than anything I could have ever imagined, each in their own special way. And if all continues as I hope it will, I'll get to see my grandbabies, and their grandbabies, and so on, though I have no intention of ever becoming my own great-great-grandson.

Nowadays, as surprising as it may be, I think of Gregor as more of a person and less of a monster. Hopefully without any sort of hindsight idealization, I combine Stan and Eileen into Gregor and think of good times we shared. See, my theory posits that after so many centuries—maybe even millennia, if "Bryn" was to be believed—Gregor no longer identified with any particular gender. I recall the countless evenings he and I spent watching our shows on

Mondays. Hardly a word spoken between us, a shared bowl of popcorn. What did Gregor get out of that? How did it play into whatever game I had imagined he was playing? Chats about philosophy, theology, and the history of daimonkind.

I think he considered me a *friend*. At some point when it was still just me and Stan—I believe, but could be wrong—I guess he wanted our relationship to grow more intimate. Stan would sometimes ask me about women, why I wasn't pursuing anyone, if a young lady from the library was still giving me the eye, stuff like that.

One day, I had screwed up the courage to ask out my colleague, Eliza, to a coffee date. It had gone as awkwardly as I expected, but all I'd told Stan was that she and I seemed to hit it off and we'd see what happens. Well, I'd forgotten all about Eliza a few days later because that's when Eileen showed up on my train. Gregor had perceived a threat.

The horrible shit? Eileen's abuse? I'm pretty sure that was just Gregor. He is not a stable entity. When Eileen would come back apologizing, I imagine now that it was genuine. I believe he truly cared, and was afraid of losing me. Further, and as much as the notion made me want to vomit all over myself and sever my penis fifty years ago, I'm confident that Gregor *loved* me.

Gender aside, this line from Congreve's *The Mourning Bride* suits Gregor perfectly:

"*Heaven has no rage like love to hatred turned, nor hell a fury like a woman scorned.*"

At my neighborhood park, my arm around my wife's waist, our kids bounding across the playground, a jogger's eyes fix on mine for an instant too long. The man's look, like myriad innocuous gestures, or sudden changes in a friend's expression or tone of voice, act as a key inserted into a music box in my mind—a discordant tune playing and echoing as Eileen's faint voice screams *Never over, Geoffrey! Never ... fucking ... over!*

*

Samuel's story continues in *Frederick & Samuel (a demons story)*

Michael Siemsen

Acknowledgements

I would like to thank my wife (and new editor), Ana, for her critical contributions to making this book what I hoped it would be. Additional editing services provided by the sharp and eagle-eyed Kristina Circelli of Red Road Editing. And as always, these stories would be nothing without my growing list of amazing beta readers: Alison C, Alyssa W, Angela P, Bill R, DeeDee B, Jessica B, Joe S, Karen L, Laura B, Laurie J, Lori W, Pascal B, Stacey L, Stephanie H, Venture C, and Vicky W—thank you all! Further thanks to Paula Margulies, Red14Films, Podium Publishing, and the late Jean-Paul Sartre, and René Descartes.

Michael Siemsen

About the Author

Michael Siemsen lives in Northern California with his wife, three kids, dog Brody, cat Atom, several fish, two chupacabrii, and one demon. He is currently spilling his guts for your entertainment.

facebook.com/mcsiemsen
michaelsiemsen.com
twitter: @michaelsiemsen
mail@michaelsiemsen.com

Also by Michael Siemsen:
A Warm Place to Call Home (a demon's story)
The Dig (Book 1 of the Matt Turner series)
The Opal (Book 2 of the Matt Turner series)

Michael Siemsen

CPSIA information can be obtained at www.ICGtesting.com
Printed in the USA
LVOW07s0319081013

355820LV00002B/6/P